THE LAST C[...]

A few cops ga[...]
on the take. [...]
day till he br[...]
sickest psycho[...]

DEDICATED TO HIS FAMILY . . .

The department was his family. Hobbes had
no wife. No girlfriend. Just his brother, Art,
and Sam, the young nephew he cherished.
They were his world and he would risk everything to keep them from harm.

DEDICATED TO THE ULTIMATE GOOD . . .

Then the killings began again and Hobbes,
the brilliant detective, could no longer doubt
the evidence. He was up against something
no one would believe. Except one haunted
woman. But by then it was too late. Those
he loved had become . . .

THE PERFECT TARGETS FOR EVIL. . . .

FALLEN

A novelization by

Dewey Gram

Based on a screenplay

written by

Nicholas Kazan

PENGUIN BOOKS

PENGUIN BOOKS

Published by the Penguin Group
Penguin Books Ltd, 27 Wrights Lane, London W8 5TZ, England
Penguin Putnam Inc., 375 Hudson Street, New York, New York 10014, USA
Penguin Books Australia Ltd, Ringwood, Victoria, Australia
Penguin Books Canada Ltd, 10 Alcorn Avenue, Toronto, Ontario, Canada M4V 3B2
Penguin Books (NZ) Ltd, 182–190 Wairau Road, Auckland 10, New Zealand

Penguin Books Ltd, Registered Offices: Harmondsworth, Middlesex, England

First published in the USA by Signet 1998
First published in Great Britain in Penguin Books 1998
1 3 5 7 9 10 8 6 4 2

PROLOGUE

A more blessed spot would be hard to find. A placid freshwater lake nestled in an old-growth hickory, maple and pine forest in the rolling mountains of an eastern state. A corner God had saved apart from earth's general mayhem. Here some lucky soul had built a pinewood log cabin among sugar maples and lilac thickets and Queen Anne's lace at the edge of the calm water. A safe haven. The only human structure for miles in any direction.

I want to tell you about the time I almost died.

The little country cabin had been constructed with rough-hewn native spruce logs and sturdy framing. A peaked roof against heavy Appalachian Range snows. Old-fashioned boxed windows with roped counterweights, twelve rectangular panes and careful caulking. A snug-fitting screen door to keep out the black flies of summer.

A cherished retreat, a place of pride.

I never thought it would happen.
Not to me. Not after all this time.

Once a place of pride.

The snug, well-built cabin was now a battered, disused hulk.

Broken panes, cobwebs, warped sideboards and split planking. Hard to imagine the owner or owners allowing their little sylvan sanctuary to fall to such ruin.

They must have had a damned good reason.

All this time alive. You get so used to living, you never dream you could die. Actually die.

Quiet. Snow-muffled ground and shrouded trees. A crisp, cold night under a starry sky.

Though the cabin hardly looked habitable, light shone inside. The reddish glare of a fire dancing up and down in the hearth.

Patches of illumination seeped out through the filthy windows and fell on the frigid ground. A broad reddish yellow swath of wavering firelight poured out the thrown open door onto the gravelly snow-covered driveway.

The crimson fire glow intermingled with the silvery moonshine and lit the scene with a bright, unreal magnesium radiance.

This appalling scene.

Beaten . . . outsmarted . . . God damn, God damn, God damn!

A man bolted away from the lighted front of the cabin across a field of carnage and into the surrounding dark.

An African-American man.

Tall, lean. In his youthful, hearty prime, but now with wild eyes, terror-filled, face glazed with sweat. He stumbled across the icy, rutted drive, lurching, clutching at his clothing. He went down on his knees, staggered up and charged on into the snow field bordering the gravel road.

The name is Hobbes. John Hobbes. The most decorated detective on the force and all that jazz.

He looked around frantically, this man Hobbes, searching with anguished eyes.

He veered and plunged toward the big trunk of a fallen fir tree and the low bushes grown up around one end of it. He dove into the bushes face first. Scrabbling with his hands, clawing the ground around them, breaking branches, he searched as though his life depended on it.

His digging became ever more ferocious, panicked, his lungs straining hoarsely for the breath of life itself.

He saw what he was after, struck at them with a desperate lunge—car keys. He snagged them, squeezed them in his fist as though to let them slip away was to lose, lose for all time.

He tried to catch his breath. Couldn't.

He tried to rise on all fours. Couldn't. He fell back into the snow and mud.

But none of the medals, hard work . . . none of it was worth a damn now.

Behind Hobbes's splayed, quivering form: the glowing windows and open door of the country cabin.

Thirty yards in the other direction: the shadow of a car half hidden back among the trees along the winding entrance road. Hobbes yearned for it, clutching the car keys, and made one last effort to rise.

Couldn't.

He spun, fell onto his back. Hyperventilating.

A face normally handsome, now twisted, ravaged by pain. He grabbed his chest in agony.

How did I get in this fix?
How did it all begin?

Quiet descended, save for the rasping, slowing breath of poor doomed bastard Hobbes.

A sudden wind picked up sheets of snow and wiped them across the driveway, working to cover the footprints and blend Hobbes's form into the landscape. The wind drew a chaste cover, too, over other fallen forms nearer the house, other signs of horror.

The wind died.

Supersaturated moonlight gave everything an eerie cast, like a photographic negative. It was no longer clear, had anyone else been there to see, what was solid substance and what was empty form, mere ephemera of light and shadow.

What *was* clear, had any other living soul been there to see and happened to be watching closely, was the thing that happened next.

What it meant, that next thing—well, that's something else again. Something that'd take some telling . . .
I'll tell you the whole damned story.
I'll tell it just the way it happened.
No, no, if I go back to the beginning, it'll take forever. Let's start more recently.
Somewhere . . . Anywhere . . .
Here.

CHAPTER 1

Edgar Reese's big night.

That's as good a place to start as any.

The designated participants were being pulled to the appointed place like iron filings to a magnet. No, like puppets by the strings of the puppet master. Reese would've liked that one better, he'd've howled.

Maximum-security state prison.

The long, high gray stone walls loomed against the oddly bright moonlit sky.

Inside, on an isolation tier within a specially quarantined wing, the man of the hour sat on his bed, propped against the pale green cell wall, waiting. Shaved head. T-shirt and prison cottons.

Edgar Reese. Multiple, aggravated, sadistic murderer.

Coolly smoking a cigarette.

The only sign of possible stress: the thick coils of smoke rising around his head from the constantly puffed cigarette.

He was being watched through the bars on three sides of his observation cell by no fewer than four guards at all times. The entire area was flooded with high-intensity white light meant to reveal any bizarre, self-damaging or suicidal behavior on the prisoner's part.

The state would not be denied.

Reese smoked on casually, face impassive, watching the clock.

They expected him to try *something*.

Reese was weird.

Bald head and eyes like shiny black olives. Sitting there statuelike. The glaring, penetrating white light heightening his weirdness. He *was* unreal, his skin almost translucent.

Outside, the windchill kicked in like a spur, the bone-cold night got colder.

The smallest details of the prison compound's towers and battlements stood out in the silvered moonlight like the hyperclear image of a postcard. The watchers took note of the odd visual effect—the congregation of watchers whose eyes were searching the edifice. It was as though their intense, unrelenting gaze itself was lighting up the cold stones.

This was the hard-case penitentiary, the place for the worst and the lost. The Reeses of the world. Few who entered in chains ever walked out free men or women, almost none. They lived out their lives, long and short, inside the walls, their deeds beyond redemption. Beyond even the notion of forgiveness.

The three dozen or so watchers—capital-punishment protesters; their numbers growing as the evening lengthened—filled the small concrete plaza across from the main entrance.

A rank of TV cameras stood stoically by, bearing witness not to the scheduled event, not even to the reactions of firsthand observers of the event, but to these arm's-length attendees. TV cameras standing eager vigil, that is, not on the violent act in the offing, but on the human emotions raised by the *idea* of the act.

Edgar Reese was slated to go out at midnight.

The departure of another sad soul from the world by official execution: It evoked a strange fascination, no matter how sad and irredeemable the soul.

Such calculated snuffing of the spark of life, even of a reduced and animalized human, was unbearable to those collected in protest. To them it was just as cruel and unholy as the acts of the condemned. A foot of flames erupted from the black-masked face of a man electrocuted in Florida earlier that same week. What could be more barbaric?

They waited in the dark, these acolytes of death and refusal—high school teacher, violinist, bank teller, dry cleaner; a woman whose mother had died within the last year, a man who had accidentally run over his own toddler son, a man whose lover was failing from AIDS; a quartet of praying seminary students, a knot of college-age louts drinking beer, an out-of-work actor studying faces. All for their own reasons awaited the snuffing of the flame.

They shuffled their feet against the cold, they chanted slogans, they held up placards and sang songs to gird themselves against the undeniable creepiness of the affair.

A group of six or eight pro-death-penalty demonstrators, some also with signs, drew together and stood facing the protestors.

These were the approvers, assembled to sanction the stark process about to take place.

These folks, for reasons ranging from keen sympathy for the victims to base bloody-mindedness, embraced the necessary evil of the state in all its civil majesty ushering a man to a bleak, just surcease. It was a stay against the dark. A reassuring excision of a cancer. Allowing that the decent and blameless might survive and flourish.

Was any human being that bad? So depraved he did not deserve the privilege of breathing in and out?

Was the man whose number was up tonight such a man?

The state's answer was embodied in a shiny green-painted metal chair—squarish, solid and utilitarian like so many things of American creation.

The death chair sat bolted to the floor in the prison execution chamber, one floor below ground at the far end of the prison compound. It was reachable by a series of long, harshly lit corridors.

The condemned would go to his death down these long windowless passageways without so much as a glimpse of the sun or the stars on his last day and night. In fact, he would not see the actual light of day at any time during his last weeks alive. To hell with him. He had forfeited even that simple human right.

A vat underneath the chair. Clean polished metal awaiting the acid, the acid that would receive the pellets. The pellets that would transmute into a choking gas that would rise up through the perforated metal seat of the chair and instantly kill anybody or anything that sucked the gas in.

Humans executing other humans—a business as old as man. The life of man was "solitary, poor, nasty, brutish and short," said a seventeenth-century philosopher. The state regularly undertook to ratify the philosopher's view with the grim bloody business of state killing.

Executions had been done through the ages in a variety of primitive ways and unprettified settings that at least had the cynical virtue of broadcasting the power and frightfulness of the act.

A stoning in the public square, a pole-axe or guillotine beheading, a raucous open-air hanging from a timber scaffold: Common criminals had to pay. Burning at the stake for heretics and witches was standard fare in the Middle Ages. Crucifixion in the Holy Roman Empire, Persia, Medieval Japan: just a public show of justice and might.

England was the bloodthirstiest: drawing and quartering. The condemned was partially strangled, and his intestines were torn out and burned while he was alive and screaming. He was silenced for good by being hacked into four parts.

That was the way executions were done, until our civilized times.

Now they were done in a bright and shining place, a clean, metallic, antiseptic facility. Herein a brisk, clinical business was conducted, was the message. No frills, no furbelows. Absolutely nothing earthy or spiritual; no returning-to-the-clay-whence-we-came folderol. Rather, a death-atorium. Impersonal, pristine.

And out of sight.

Modern America did its social cleansing out of the public eye, discreetly. To spare us the primal, bottom-dwelling horror.

And more power to us, that we kept our killing at a distance and did not choose to wallow in the deaths we decreed. That was what made us civilized, after all, wasn't it?

CHAPTER 2

Death was on schedule so far this night. The second hand on the clock inside the wan green execution chamber swept round and round, pushing the minutes, advancing the hours. Squeezing the time for living into smaller and smaller increments.

Edgar Reese sat on the bed, his legs stretched out comfortably, in his segregated observation cell at the opposite end of the same sequestered wing. He was watching the dwindling minutes tick by on the wall clock opposite his cage.

Cigarette in his left hand, a long drag. Through the swirl of smoke Reese saw the minute hand jolt another small notch closer to twelve.

Life was dwindling down, heartbeats remaining numbered in the mere thousands.

But from the evidence of the man's eyes, the mind within the shaved skull was not slowing nor musing on last things. It was racing. Angry, vengeful. Plotting, despite the hard fact of the approaching end. The idea of peaceful resignation and acceptance of fate was a laugh to this dying man.

A uniformed guard passed by. Rattlesnake strike: Reese jumped for the barred door. Metal cracked against metal sharp as a gunshot. The guard startled.

"Hey, shithead," Reese hissed, "where's Hobbes?"

The guard looked at him and walked on.

Reese watched him go with a smirk.

Reese was young, just turned thirty, with a lean, conditioned build. Vital-looking. His mind was sharp, his appetites bursting. Free, he'd be entering the shank of his days, his greatest pleasures and satisfactions still ahead.

Fuck that, said the man's face. Fuck any lame weep-weeping over losses, this dude was not going to waste his energy. He was not going to wail and rue his dwindling wedge of time. Instead, he smirked and shrieked again for Hobbes.

Some people chewed at the ends of their fingers, smoked cigarettes, twisted their hair or mustache. A half-dollar piece was Hobbes's worry bead. His habitual plaything for soothing his nerves or doing deep thinking.

Most of the time he didn't even know he was doing it. Now he knew. He was consciously twiddling his half-dollar to keep the queasiness at bay.

Queasiness was standard for Hobbes at this stage of an execution; not open anxiety, more an uneasy feeling and a clenched state of mind. He would not begin to relax until it was over, many days over.

He stood in a courtyard just inside the main gates to the prison, waiting. Above him searchlights crept along the stone walls, and the preternaturally bright moonlight chromed the tops of the towers.

A tall man in a trench coat, holding two cups of coffee, pushed through a crowd of newspeople and approached Hobbes.

William Stanton, Hobbes's boss. A tough, smart cookie whose ash white bristle-cut hair and dour ex-

pression gave him the look of a Marine DI saddled
with a company of wimp slackers.

Stanton was more than a nail-splitting DI, though.
An intelligent, surprisingly humane look about the
eyes cut against the Marine look. And confused people. They never knew which Stanton to expect, the
thoughtful smiling humanist or the hard-ass. Stanton
took full advantage. He was comfortable keeping the
other guy on edge.

He moved up next to Hobbes and handed him a
coffee as a limo pulled up in the driveway outside
the gates.

Hobbes nodded his thanks for the coffee. They both
took note of the somber-faced cashmere-topcoated self-
important man who emerged. "The governor?" Hobbes
said to Stanton. "I thought he didn't approve."

"The more they don't approve, the more they want
to watch," Stanton said. "So what's this, six notches
on your belt?"

Stanton knew the answer; it was a friendly tease.
In the background, the governor and his aide but-
toned their coats and walked through the prison
gates.

"Eight," Hobbes said.

Stanton gave his trademark slightly ironic smile:
"Congratulations."

"Fuck you," Hobbes said. But friendly. These two
had a long history. "Fuck you" was an endearment
between cops who'd worked closely and amicably
together for more than a decade.

"Ask more nicely, huh?" Stanton joked dryly. Neither of them savored this gig one bit. Any and all
attempts at cutting through the pall and lightening
up the spirits were in order.

A prison aide opened the inside door, stepped out

and flicked a look at Hobbes. "He wants you in the dance hall," he barked. Even the guards were off their feed tonight. Not even the toughest screw was indifferent to the doings the night of a smoker.

Hobbes glanced at Stanton, rolled his eyes. He stepped toward the prison, pulling his coat closer around his shoulders.

CHAPTER 3

Hobbes approached through a dimly lit cellblock, through streaks of light and darkness. The pattern of bars fell across his face as he walked, his footsteps echoing. A vacant tier, kept empty as a buffer lest anxiety or hysteria from the condemned spread like a contagion throughout the prison.

Hobbes slowed and stopped in deep shadow next to a young cameraman's assistant reloading some film equipment in the hallway. He looked inside the brightly lit cell area. Two young filmmakers with backwards baseball caps were shooting Reese, who was puffing intently on a cigarette.

Reese brightened at the sight of Hobbes, came alive. "Well, well," he said. He gestured at Hobbes for the filmmakers' sake. "The brilliant detective who sealed my brutish fate." He smirked at Hobbes. "I thought you'd be too cowardly to show."

Hobbes motioned for the guard to let him into the containment pen. As the guard did so, Hobbes checked out the camera guys. "What's this, somebody makin' you famous?"

"Big time!" Reese said, rolling off his bunk, coming to the bars. "They're putting me in the movies, pal. Documentary. Courtesy of the ACLU: They're gonna shoot me getting smoked." He went into an exaggerated death pose, gagging, tongue out, then flopping his head over dead. "Could be a big video rental. Society ladies showin' it at dinner parties . . ." He took on a high voice: "You see that? They tell me that's a *urine* stain. . . ."

He smiled, flipped back to his normal voice. "It's good to see you, Hobbes."

"It's good to be seen by you, Reese," Hobbes said with a smile, pulling up a chair across from the condemned man.

Reese suddenly and aggressively stuck his hand through the bars. "My best pal. Shake?"

Hobbes looked at the hand. What was this, some kind of trick? The pathetic attempt of a defanged hyena to give him a scare? Well, if it was, Hobbes was more than ready, more than capable. He leaned forward from his chair opposite the cell and coolly shook Reese's hand, watching his eyes.

Reese looked out at him through the bars, tilted his head as though sensing something, and murmured, "Still a good boy." He started to squeeze and fondle Hobbes's hand as though trying to get something from it—comfort, power?

Hobbes yanked his hand back. "Hey, I'm not your priest," he said.

Reese gave a fierce grin. "Sure you are," he said, then launched into a long, wacko dirge of some kind, nonsense syllables, fast and unintelligible, muttered under his breath.

Hobbes watched, his patience strained. "I hope you're having fun," he said.

Reese flew into a sudden pantomime. He "touched" the air, "fucked" his fist with his index finger, rubbed his palms together. Energetic, outlandish, peculiar. Not particularly directed toward Hobbes, not provocative in that way. Just damned peculiar.

Hobbes shook his head, but before he could speak, Reese slid smoothly into intelligible language again. "You remind me of someone, Hobbes. Indeed you do. Do you like riddles?"

Hobbes looked at him and said wearily, "Nope."

"Here's a beaut," Reese said. "Why is there a space between Lyons and Spakowsky?"

"I give up," Hobbes said, bored.

"You should *know* this one," Reese snapped with a nasty smile. "Open your eyes, pal. Look around sometime."

The cameras whirred in the background, recording the queer kind of give and take Reese chose for one of his last conversations.

Hobbes shook his head in disgust and moved toward the containment pen door.

Reese pressed against the bars, his voice suddenly strong and commanding. "Remember this, Hobbes," he barked. "In a day, a week, month. Remember: *Wie wind zaait, zal storm oogsten.*"

"What're you, a Nazi now?" Hobbes said.

Reese smirked condescendingly: "It's Dutch."

"Meaning?"

"What goes around . . . *really goes around,*" Reese blurted emphatically.

Hobbes gave a half laugh. "Have a safe trip, hear?" he said. He walked out.

Behind him Reese called, "I'll be looking for you!" He performed some more dancelike contortions and spouted more gibberish.

Hobbes waited out in the shadowy cell block, alone with his thoughts. He had done his duty toward the man, he felt: given him his last shot, let him work out a little for whatever it was worth, whatever solace it might have provided.

Hobbes always had some fellow feeling, despite himself, for the condemned men he'd sent up, as they went to their reward. And always a twinge of some unnameable feeling for his part in their final journey. It wasn't guilt, it wasn't responsibility for their fate. It was a weight of some kind though, undeniably.

With Reese, Hobbes felt almost none of that fellow feeling. Nor did he feel implicated in the man's approaching demise in the usual unspecifiable way. Still, he felt uneasy. Reese was so singularly strange, he left a powerful impression of . . . what?

The time was drawing nigh.

The officers came to exchange Reese's prison cottons and T-shirt for a one-piece yellow-orange jumpsuit, the easier to zip his body out once he was a corpse.

They put Reese in leg and wrist irons and waist chains and then unlocked the cell. As they marched him out, he began humming rather jauntily. As they led him down the long, garishly lit corridor, through one set of clanking sliding doors after another, Reese continued to sing, buoyantly and unintelligibly. And he danced, in time to his own singing. He danced jiglike and lightheartedly—how else to say it—all the way down the spooky, echoing hallway leading to his doom.

CHAPTER 4

The gas chamber was a hermetically sealed, eight-sided, large-windowed enclosure at one end of an observation room. Adjoining it was the control room, where the guards, prison doctor, county medical examiner and death technicians waited and worked.

In the viewing room opposite the chamber, the chairs were lined up for VIP witnesses and selected press; for family and friends of the condemned and for the families of victims if they chose to attend.

The octagonal death chamber itself was just a few yards square. Witnesses would be seated quite close to the convicted killer when the moment of reckoning came. They could stand right at the windows and be just six or seven feet away if they had the stomach for the grisly minutiae of death.

Final preparations were under way. Several guards, including a round-faced, clean-cut young redheaded corrections officer, followed a checklist of last-minute duties.

The redheaded officer, Jimmy Rourke, had the fit, sturdy look of a high school athlete just a few years out of school. It was he who checked the death chair: hand, leg and ankle straps, the metal vat, the acid supply and pellet delivery system.

Another officer carefully smeared Vaseline over the

rubber seals around the observation windows and door. He checked the operation of the venetian blinds.

A technician readied the supplies of caustic soda and anhydrous ammonia for swabbing down the chamber afterward.

A guard brought some additional folding chairs into the viewing area and arranged them. He tested the telephone to make sure it was an open line to the prison switchboard, in the event of a last-minute stay of execution from the U.S. Court of Appeals or the U.S. Supreme Court.

A last-minute stay was never impossible, even for an Edgar Reese. Stays were more the rule than the exception in the eighties and early nineties. The Supreme Court, after having voided all state and federal death penalty laws in 1972, was now ruling that rewritten state capital punishment laws were constitutional. State governments, having become unaccustomed to pulling the trigger, delayed for a while, but now they had gotten their nerve back. The pace had steadily increased until more than fifty felons were frying each year by the mid-nineties.

Seemed like a lot, but it wasn't nearly enough to deplete the death-row crowd. There was a backlog of three thousand condemned killers, mostly men, with three hundred more added to the waiting list each year. It was not the best of times in the U.S. of A., to judge by the numbers. It was not the peaceable kingdom.

Edgar Reese had been on the Row, and had been running through various appeals, for six years. Not a particularly long time considering some condemned men dragged out their appeals for twenty years before giving up the ghost.

But Reese was swimming against the tide. The courts and the voters had said enough was enough. Reese's string, barring divine intervention, had almost surely run out.

The phone would not be ringing.

Rourke, the red-haired guard, loaded the supply of sulfuric acid. He hooked up the little gauze bag stuffed with sodium cyanide pellets that hung above the acid vat on a metal link chain. The instruments were ready for the deadly intermingling.

Rourke checked his watch, walked back into the technician's room and unlocked the executioner's buttons and silver-handled release lever on the control panel.

The VIPs and families began to file in. Thirty-one in all.

Most of them were stone-faced relatives of Reese's victims. One group was the family of one of the Arab boys Reese had killed. He had left behind evidence at the Arab boys' murders that Jewish militants had committed the atrocities.

The one boy's family used their life savings to come from Jordan: father, mother and two brothers. They were looking for relief from their fury and grief, even now six years later.

The murdered son had been the family's hope. An eighteen-year-old math prodigy, he had led the Jordanian team at the International Mathematical Olympiad in Roumania, and in the process won a full scholarship, living stipend and research grant at the university in Hobbes's city. He was a freshman getting A's in graduate-level math courses when Reese singled him out.

Reese was thorough, methodical, patient. He spotted the handsome foreign-looking boy and followed him for several days around the campus, observing, looking for the keyhole to unlock the young man's trust. He found it: The young man doted on dogs, petted them, yearned for one of his own. Reese brought a German shepherd puppy to a street bordering the campus and waited. He broke the dog's leg when he saw the Arab boy coming, and he easily got the boy to hold the dog in his arms while Reese drove them "to the hospital."

The boy was found dead eight days later in a recycling bin with a Star of David carved on his chest.

The dog was found dead in a dumpster elsewhere in the city on the same day, skinned alive, and its neck wrung. The dog, ironically, was Hobbes's key to nailing Reese.

The seventy-third student Hobbes questioned mentioned a man with a dog. The same day Hobbes happened to overhear two morgue technicians talking about a murdered puppy. The student picked the dead German shepherd puppy from a dead dog lineup. At the seventeenth pet shop Hobbes visited, the owner i.d.-ed the dog and gave Hobbes enough leads to the buyer that Hobbes eventually caught up with Reese. And found the dead boy's DNA on Reese's torture and carving tools.

There was no family present in the viewing chamber for Reese. The addict father, who had beat him for laziness and burned his genitals with cigarettes for wetting the bed, had long since disappeared from his life.

Reese's mother had died from alcohol poisoning when he was six.

His father fed him only once every other day, to toughen him and because he looked like he'd "run to fat" if he ate daily. He made the boy masturbate for his women friends to show what a little man he was. He kneeled on the boy's throat and pissed in his mouth for talking back.

Reese joined the Marines at age seventeen, intending to become a killing machine and off his father. He was court-martialed for rape and assault in his first year of duty, imprisoned and dishonorably discharged.

After another hitch in the pen for attempted robbery, he got a job as a bus driver and on the surface went straight. He haunted the library and got a high school equivalency diploma on his own. He had a clean record at work, except that he was suspected of running over pets for sport.

He started killing people four years before he got caught. A street kid made the mistake of offering him sex for twenty dollars, then asking too many questions about the burn marks all around his genitals. The kid was asking to get his anus burned with an iron and his neck broken, and to be dropped off the bridge into the river.

The Arab youths were numbers six, seven and eight. But for Hobbes's efforts, ten or twelve more unsuspecting souls might have met grisly deaths by this night. But for Hobbes's grind-it-out, two-yards-and-a-cloud-of-dust style of police work, and his mulish belief that the young Arabs' deaths weren't political at all, Reese would have spread his mayhem far wider.

The balding, grim-visaged governor entered the death chamber. He held his head high as though that were the correct posture for signaling distaste for the proceedings while still manfully doing the people's bidding.

The warden, a craggy, stocky man in his mid-fifties wearing his formal double-breasted gray suit, walked in beside him. He looked about as happy as a teamster going before a congressional subcommittee to testify. He took his place close to the glass, where he could signal the technicians when the moment came.

The three-member press pool took their places by a window—print, TV and radio—all men. No cameras or recording equipment allowed. The priest stood dutifully ready to transmit his final blessing through the glass to the departing soul.

The documentary camera crew entered, filming as they came.

Hobbes and Stanton walked in and stood, coats on, hands in pockets, shoulders hunched, as though the whole proceeding were being conducted out in the icy night wind.

The clock read: 11:57.

CHAPTER 5

Things now moved at almost split-second intervals.

Reese in his clinking leg, arm and waist chains was led briskly by the guards into the gas chamber through the rear door. Orange jumpsuit and soft hospital-type slippers; shaved, defiant head shiny with sweat.

Jimmy Rourke, the redheaded guard, followed him in. Rourke was alert, all business. No telling what a man will do as his wick burns down the last inch.

Simultaneously, guards at either side snapped open the venetian blinds shielding the interior of the chamber from the viewing room.

Reese spread his arms wide at the sight of the gathered. "Howdy, ladies. Gents. Cocksuckers and pederasts," he said loudly. "Hope you like the show." He blew a kiss. "Hello, Gov, my love."

"He's certainly enjoying himself," the governor said in an irritated aside to the warden, never taking his eyes off the leering convict.

"Always has," the warden said. "That's why we're so pleased to see him graduate."

The accompanying guards grabbed Reese's arms, putting an end to the show. They turned him and led him to the chair, sat him down. His defiant, arrogant smile never faltered as the guards strapped him into the chair.

Officer Rourke watched from the doorway. When the first two guards finished their quick work and retreated, Rourke stepped forward. While the prison doctor was quickly attaching electrodes to Reese's chest for the EKG, Rourke checked the ankle straps, then put his hands over the wrist straps, making sure they were secure.

Reese's left hand flipped over and grabbed Rourke's hand. A vise grip. The redhead showed no surprise, he just looked down at the grasping hand.

Reese whispered hoarsely: "I'll give you a blow job if you get me out of this."

Gotcha! Rourke recoiled in disgust, grossed out despite himself. He'd seen lots of sick fucks in his day, but never one as strange and sick as Reese.

Reese laughed—mindfuck! He let go of Rourke's hand.

Rourke stepped back, moved quickly out of the chamber and entered the technician's cubicle. He sat behind the small control panel. He was the man in control—the official executioner.

Rourke had drawn the "smoke-Reese" duty in a random draw from a small pool of correction officer volunteers. There was a pay premium for performing the nerve-rattling duty: five hundred dollars.

A guard sealed the door. Rourke turned a knob and watched the needle on the air-pressure gauge go up until it indicated positive air pressure on the outside of the chamber.

The prison doctor stood near the heart monitor.

Rourke glanced at the clock: 11:59. Sixty seconds and counting: The time to earn his bonus was upon him.

In the gas chamber Reese's lips started to move.

In the viewing room the witnesses heard a sound

coming from the condemned man, its volume steadily increasing.

The governor frowned. "What's he doing?" he said to the warden.

The warden's assistant, a bland-faced younger man whom the warden had assigned to monitor Reese closely in the final weeks, spoke up. "He's . . . I believe he's singing, sir," he said. The warden's assistant wasn't surprised at anything Reese did, having seen a steadily mounting stream of cuckoo behavior and unintelligible spoutings as the time neared.

"Time . . . is on my side. . . . Yes, it is," Reese sang loudly.

The Rolling Stones song. Raucous, gravelly, right on key. An astonishing sound—and sentiment—to be coming out of a man who knew himself to be within seconds of death.

"Time . . . is on my side. . . . You know it is . . ." he wailed, scanning the crowd, his audience, with evident delight at their awed, uncertain reactions.

The governor, enraged by the spectacle, glanced at the clock. The sweep second hand closed in on 12, almost midnight. He caught the eye of his aide holding the phone with the open line to his ear. No call from the courts to postpone.

Reese grinned and kept at it. "You always said you wanna be free. . . ." A maniac with good pipes. He looked through the glass straight at Hobbes.

Hobbes shook his head. He couldn't help smiling at the madness of it all. In the fingers of his right hand a silver coin rotated around and around.

Reese crooned, "I'll come runnin' back. . . . I'll come runnin' back. . . . Like I have so many times before . . ."

The governor elbowed the warden: *Do it!*

Yes, of course, the warden's half nod said. But his eyes were on the clock; nothing could happen until the second hand hit 12.

Reese sang away as if it were just another day in the life. "Go ahead! Light up my life!" he howled.

CHAPTER 6

The second hand swept toward the vertical and hit it. Midnight. The warden nodded toward the executioner's cubicle.

In the cubicle the impassive-faced Rourke reached with his right hand, grasped the release lever and pulled. No hesitation. Don't even think about it, he'd been counseled by other men who had done it. Think about anything else in the moments approaching— baseball, his girlfriend, what his last car repair had cost. And then, when he got the nod, be in a hurry to pull the stick. The quicker the better.

In the gas chamber the gauze bag of yellowish sodium cyanide pellets on its little chain slid down into the waiting acid under the chair. Greenish white sulphur cyanide gas billowed up the instant the pellets hit, thin at first, then thicker and oilier.

Reese held his breath, fifteen seconds, half a minute, cheeks bulging, as the gas rose sensuous and deadly around him. He leered at the audience through the shimmering vapors, turning his head, scanning back and forth, face to face to face, as though memorizing them for wreaking vengeance from beyond.

Fifty seconds, a minute—an eternity to the watchers. Would this never end?

Reese, wild-eyed and satanic with fumes coursing

and boiling up past his head, took joy in dragging out the ugly suspense, joy in extending this final moment of holding some fraction of humankind in horrible thrall. The same kind of exquisite joy he took in his slow, torturous killings.

The faces of some of the women witnesses began to tremble from the awful tension, verging toward tears.

Reese saw and exulted.

Then, running out of oxygen, of time, of choices— veins standing out on his head—he puckered. And, with a vast exhalation of held-in air, blew them all a kiss. He violently sucked in the poison.

His body jerked one way, then the other, his chest heaved convulsively. His head snapped back and quivered for several seconds. His eyes bugged, wide open. Then his head eased forward. He was still.

A ribbon of drool oozed out of his mouth.

In the viewing area the faces of the observers registered a kaleidoscope of human reaction. Repelled, excited, transfixed. Emotions poured through them like a wild electric current.

Death: Sudden, abrupt, final. It lurks for all of us, just around the corner, a breath away.

Yes, but which corner? Which breath?

After a long moment their expressions changed. Men and women both. The meter on their keen, expectant, angry, grieving eyes went down to zero.

Shocked aftermath.

It was over so fast. To a person, the witnesses suddenly felt drained, as though, in leaving, Reese had sucked the air out of the room.

Stanton's face was gray. His usually clear, sharp

eyes were out of focus. He took a deep breath and glanced at Hobbes.

Hobbes just stared through the window at the dead meat that had been such a packet of jokey, mocking energy only seconds before.

The slab of meat, slumped forward in the chair, wasn't done, however. One of the women, mother of a girl Reese had killed, happened to glance down at one of Reese's clenched hands, his left hand, at the moment the pinkie finger moved. It *moved*. She felt herself going faint, grabbed onto her companion.

Just a final muscular twitch, she reassured herself, just a last nerve reflex.

In the executioner's cubicle stalwart redheaded point man Rourke maintained his steely impassivity as he watched Reese's face and noted the flat line on the EKG. But on the inside, Rourke was jazzed: He'd done it, he'd pulled the kill switch and hadn't flinched. It had cost him *nothing*. He was one tough motherfucker.

Reese's face, bent down, was not visible to most of the witnesses. Good thing. His eyes were open, and he did not look dead. Downright creepy.

But Hobbes, over at the side, *could* see. From that angle, Reese's tilted, bent-over head gave the impression that the now-rigid man was looking out of the corner of his eye at the police detective. Casting a mordant eye at the man who brought him to this end.

Stop yourself, Hobbes said to himself. He tore his eyes away from the collapsed body in the chair and glanced around at the other witnesses. As he did, he experienced an odd effect: Sound became distant, muted. A cough, the scrape of a chair on the floor, somebody blowing his nose. All as though happen-

ing in some parallel reality removed from his own.
No: as though *he* was suddenly removed from their
shared reality and was observing it from outside.

The transmigration of souls.

Do *souls really migrate?*

Is *death really final, or does something move? Does
something pass?*

*It's hard for most people to believe that at the instant
of death comes total extinction, but if something does
move, where does it move* to? *If something does pass,
who does it pass to? Again, most people think they'll never
get an answer to questions like these.*

Keep reading.

Hobbes looked at the warden, moved his eyes over
to the governor, then glanced at Stanton standing
beside him. All seemed different, estranged.

Then he peered across into the cubicle, where the
redheaded executioner was going about his work.
Hobbes looked for comfort there, in the procedural
minutiae, in the routine performance of duties.

Comforting at first, yes. Then no comfort.

For as he watched Rourke's face, he saw a look of
harsh triumph pass over it, and there was something
eerily recognizable about the look. Then it was gone.
Suddenly, even the dull functionary gave Hobbes the
willies. Snap out of it, he said to himself. Get a grip.

Inside his cubicle Rourke checked the time and jotted a few notes in his official logbook. The door
opened behind him, and the warden stuck his head
in. The governor was standing a few feet away.

"You okay, Jimmy?" the warden said.

"Yeah, sure," Rourke said, adding with a hint of
admiration, "Never saw one sing before."

"Me, neither," the warden said.

Across in the viewing area Hobbes was watching

through the glass as the warden closed the door and Rourke smiled to himself. There: that hint of something again, the recognizable look, just for an instant.

Hobbes shook himself. He shifted his feet impatiently, waiting for the drains and exhaust valves to open and suck up and neutralize the lethal gas and clear the chamber. So the medical examiner could perform the laying on of hands and declare Edgar Reese officially dead. Officially removed from the rolls of creatures who walked the land with the prime purpose of casting fury and carnage wherever they went.

CHAPTER 7

Hobbes and Stanton exited the prison along with the other witnesses and walked toward their cars. Gray-faced. No small talk. No more gallows humor. It always took a while to wind down.

Reporters swarmed to them, yammered around them, scrambling for details, looking for quotes. Some were filing stories for the late news as they hurried along, talking to minicams or into their cell phones:

". . . pronounced dead at 12:18 . . ."

". . . thirty-one witnesses . . ."

". . . One of the worst prisoners in the history of the state. . ."

A blond local TV correspondent did a standup before a live minicam, trying to give her pretty face as much gravity as possible. "While he was inside, Reese started destructive fires, triggered a riot, and founded a KKK unit . . ."

Local TV news star Harvey Rosenstein recognized Police Detective Hobbes and motioned his cameraman to swing over. He pushed a mike in front of Hobbes's face as he fell in beside him. "Why do you come, Detective? Why do you watch?" His manner was characteristically self-important and baiting. "Lieutenant Stanton has to be here to hold hands with the governor, but what?—you get pleasure out of watching?"

Hobbes answered without rising to the bait. He knew Rosenstein well enough to expect, and ignore, his hard-charger manner. "Criminals don't accept consequences," Hobbes said evenly. "They kill somebody? Somehow it's not their fault. This is the consequence of what I do; I better be here."

That was just the headline of what drove Hobbes to be there, of course, but he knew from experience it was all the local news wanted, a stand-alone soundbite. Punchy and resolute. Something that sounded like an *answer*.

A fuller explanation of his reasons would include harder-to-summarize matters: his own complex ambivalence about the death penalty; his professional need to plant graphic reminders in his forebrain never to accept pat or easy answers in his investigation of capital cases, given the potential deadly outcome; his will to do his part in lending gravity to a proceeding that some people wanted to cheer and celebrate.

And on a personal and private level, Hobbes harbored the instinct that watching the official machinery of death grind up a human being would prevent him from ever being self-pitying about how tough his own life was.

He turned away from the clutch of reporters. And as he did, the governor appeared from inside the prison, and the reporters rushed off in his direction.

Stanton looked at Hobbes. "Yeah, but it's *not* your fault," he said in his dry and friendly manner.

Hobbes smiled, appreciating it, gave Stanton a friendly cuff with the back of his hand.

"Goin' home?" Stanton said, offering a ride.

"Nah," Hobbes said. "Some of the guys wanna ride me about Reese." He laughed. "The cop who brought the mad dog to heel, savior of cities, the mountie what always gets his man. The usual shit . . . I could stand a couple of belts." He shook his head ruefully at the memory of what had just occurred.

Driving slowly toward them in a vintage red Cadillac convertible was Jimmy Rourke, the executioner, now in civilian dress. Relaxed, heading out. He gave Hobbes and Stanton a casual glance. They would probably not have even noticed him, except that as he passed they heard him singing. It was what he was singing: "Always" by Irving Berlin.

Just a beautiful night and a happy guy who did a good job of work and was looking forward to the next day off.

Hobbes and Stanton stared after Jimmy.

". . . but always . . . All the time . . ."

CHAPTER 8

Castle Street. The downtown club and entertainment quarter, where rock joints, strip bars, steakhouses and video arcades stayed open all night and attracted crowds bent on scoring, unwinding, jamming, just hanging.

Jimmy Rourke parked his big red boat on a neon-lit block and got out. He stretched his legs walking along the teeming street, enjoying watching the people, taking immense pleasure in the aliveness of it all. Immense *perverse* pleasure, so said the odd expression on his round face.

He ordered a burger at a stand, paid for it and walked along eating it, eyeing people. Then an incident, very small, almost nothing; Jimmy couldn't even say for sure what it was. Just a weird sense of *something* . . .

Something is always happening. But when it happens, people don't always see it, don't always know it.

Don't always accept it.

Why? Why is that some people resist. Most people give in.

Jimmy raised his arm to take a bite, and his elbow brushed against a Japanese businessman coming the other way. Jimmy walked on, three steps, four; then abruptly slowed and almost stopped. He looked around as though momentarily lost. He looked at his burger curiously for half a beat.

Then he walked on, more slowly. He sank his teeth into the burger and realized how good it tasted. He picked up his jaunty pace again, relishing the food in his mouth and the vibrancy of his surroundings.

But the Japanese businessman . . .

A crisp efficient walker swinging an attaché case. Trim, ordinary-looking, middle-aged Asian wearing his street face: inscrutable.

Until the moment of being touched.

His face changed then—very slightly, subtly—but changed. It would be hard to label the transformation, but a sharp light seemed to appear in his eyes.

But only for just the space of a few steps along the pavement.

In overtaking and passing a young couple, the Japanese businessman rubbed shoulders with a handsome buzz-cut college kid, nineteen, who was holding hands with his beautiful long-legged girlfriend in a denim microskirt. The couple abruptly veered and cut into the street in the middle of the block.

As they ignored the cruising cars and neared the other side, they came face-to-face with three muscle-builders in puce green muscle-tees just stepping off the curb. The beautiful girlfriend flagrantly bumped against the biggest of them and kept walking, ignoring the contact.

The young muscle-builder turned, looked, took a few steps backwards as he made his way across the street with his homies.

He faced front and scanned the crowd on the sidewalk ahead of him. He focused on an almost anorexic young man in a long, untucked brown shirt who stepped off the curb. He was carrying a take-out food bag across the street toward the miniature golf course. A meek-faced guy, the anorexic, not a lot going on behind the eyes; just doing a job delivering food.

Very purposefully, the muscle-builder reached out and touched the thin delivery guy's arm. The thin guy didn't even look at the muscled guy; just lengthened his stride and straightened his back a little as he moved on.

A thin smile came to his face.

He walked on to the mini golf course. He passed through the open double doors, walked up to the counter and half tossed the take-out food bag in front of the owner.

Harry Moohr was a crusty ex-military lifer who had bought this joint for his retirement, thinking he was going to enjoy raking in the dollars and talking to the nice people. Instead, he was losing money to a mountain of city fees, taxes, insurance, and fighting constantly with abusive teenagers. He was pretty much hating every second he had to work here.

Still, he was a generous-hearted guy and good boss who had given the young, nearly anorexic fellow, Charles, a job when others had found him too distracted of thought and slow of foot. Charles had been surprisingly reliable and deferential.

Harry had not had a good night, though, at the mini golf. The gang-bangers had been relentlessly loutish. "Dammit, Charles," Harry said, "what took you so long? That girl over on the thirteenth hole dropped an earring in the water wheel, and she's standing there waiting—"

"You know what you'd look like with this sand-

wich up your ass?'' Charles said blandly, pulling the
sandwich out of the bag and holding it up.

Harry reacted. ''Pardon me??''

''Like a fat stupid fuck with a sandwich up his
ass,'' Charles said with a short laugh.

Harry just about swallowed his gum. This wasn't
the meek, well-mannered Charles who showed up
every day grateful to have a paying job. ''Charles,''
he said, ''I hate to do this, but—''

Charles flipped him off. ''Put the job where the
sandwich goes,'' he said. He gave a sarcastic snort
and walked off. Walked with a different stride than
Harry remembered him having. Almost a swagger.

CHAPTER 9

The Dugout was a cop bar in the mixed black-white-Hispanic-Armenian neighborhood under the elevated train behind the precinct. It was run by an Irish ex-cop named Ricardo Boyd.

Dick Boyd, like every ex-cop, had a story: retired on disability when another cop on a raid accidentally shot him in the left arm and ruined his elbow. He could barely bend the arm, it was true, but really all it had done was improve his golf swing. And bank account.

For a while he'd worked as a car paint distributor, but he got bored and he missed the men. So, over his wife, Sheila's, objections, he put most of his fat disability settlement into this bar and continued to serve the force, in a different way. It was working out great financially—Sheila was solid with that. But now Dick was *never* home. He took his loyalties seriously: His fellow cops needed him.

One of his favorites came through the front door—Hobbes. Looking worn down.

Like every other cop on the force, Dick knew what was coming down that night and had been expecting to see Hobbes. He raised his chin in time-honored greeting to a regular. He signaled with his eyes toward the tables in the back, throwing a knowing roll of his eyes in with it, meaning: Watch yourself, trouble ahead. All with both hands immersed in water washing out beer glasses. A casual observer wouldn't have been sure any communication had taken place at all.

Hobbes nodded and made his way toward the back, ignoring the TV playing over the bar: news shots of Reese from his long-ago trial. Then a shot of milling protesters with a sign: BURN REESE BURN. A quick cut to Hobbes himself being interviewed.

That Hobbes could do without.

He threaded his way toward a rear table where he saw Lou, Tiffany, Lawrence and Jonesy. Tiffany and Lawrence were standing up, putting on their coats. The table was littered with empty beer bottles. They all raised their glasses as Hobbes hove into sight.

"There he is, man of the hour," said Lou. Lou La-Cava was a thickset veteran with a heavy black mustache. He was the kind of guy who led with his mouth and was always ready to throw the first punch. Especially when loaded, as he was now.

"Mr. Consequences," said Tiffany, teasing Hobbes about his TV interview. She was a short Italian woman about thirty with curly black hair and nine years experience as a cop. She was as hard-nosed and physically tough as any of the males. She had a tougher Italo-American accent and was better looking than all of them.

"Yeah, yeah, yeah," Hobbes said. "Where're you going?"

"We waited," Tiffany said. "We drank a round in your honor, then two more, now I gotta break the law just to drive home."

"Get off it, Tiffany," Lawrence said. "Our cab is here." Lawrence was a trim, wiry cop with an Italian wise-guy look, slicked-back black hair, a shiny black leather car coat. He was forty years old and five years away from his "twenty-and-done."

Tiffany came around the table. "Well then, congrats," she said. She kissed Hobbes on the cheek and started away. "Don't get drunk and disorderly, you hear?"

Hobbes smiled, waved, sat.

Jonesy half grinned at him and started a quick exchange—of a different quality, that of partners. More than friends.

"So? How was it?" Jonesy asked.

"He died."

"Told you," Jonesy said, comedian.

Jonesy was a great-looking guy—big, chubby-cheeked, easygoing smile, friendliest puss this side of the circus. He had ham hands made for clapping guys on the back and giving kids hugs. But he was substantially overweight, getting more so. And he smoked. A worry to his partner and fellow officers. He swore to change his eating and smoking habits every day. Every day!

Lou grabbed the passing waitress. "Hey, Gracie," he said, "we got one more."

Jonesy blew smoke from his cigarette; it billowed near Hobbes.

"Please, huh?" Hobbes said, waving the smoke away. "Don't tempt me." He pushed Jonesy's pack of smokes farther away from him on the table. Hobbes had quit two years before; he wished Jonesy would quit, too, for his health's sake. Who was he to grind on him?

"What's your poison, Hobbes?" Gracie said, amiable. Gracie was a hard-working single mother pushing thirty, not bad-looking, but no three-alarm fire.

Curly auburn hair that was always falling over her eyes, having to be tucked behind her ears. She was friendly but not flirty. Having bedded a number of cops in earlier years, she'd learned it never worked out. Now, raising two kids and trying to sustain a romantic relationship with a Greek club owner named Paul, she needed no one-night stands with horny cops to spoil the moussaka, thank you very much.

Lou did a table inventory for Hobbes's benefit. "We been working on Bass ales, a Beck's, a Guinness—" He put a welcoming arm around Gracie's waist as she waited. He had designs; he didn't know from any Greek club owner.

"I'll have a Bud," Hobbes said.

"A Bud?" Lou said with exaggerated condescension.

"Yeah," Hobbes said.

"We're goin' imported here," Lou said grandly. "You can't afford, I'll treat."

"I can afford," Hobbes said dryly.

"At least get a Bud Ice, huh?" Lou insisted.

Hobbes shook his head.

"Bud Lite? Bud Extra Dry? Keep me interested." Lou was drunk, flying treetop level, on a roll.

But more than that: Lou was baiting Hobbes; Lou was being an asshole.

Hobbes wasn't going to bite, though, wasn't going to descend to that level. He just gave a straightforward answer. "Bud."

"It's just a Bud, Lou, okay?" Gracie said impatiently, pulling free of his grasp. She left, irritated with him for wasting her time.

Lou, his fantasies of side action with Gracie dealt a palpable blow, took his annoyance out on Hobbes. He selected a needle and stuck it in. "You're an unusual cop, Hobbes," he said. "Let me ask you something, huh?'' Lou relished this kind of passive aggressive goading. "I've only been in your precinct what, six months?" he said, "but they say you never take cream, is that true?" He put on a look of fake sincerity.

A subtle tightening on Jonesy's part: A taboo subject had been spoken aloud.

But Lou seemed completely cool, relaxed. He was ripped, out on the high wire, and he enjoyed being totally casual about it.

A welcome diversion.

Jack Fergusen, an old friend of Hobbes's father, stopped by the table. He was a retired fire captain, a regular at the bar. "You were good, Johnny, on the tube," he said. "Your dad'd be proud."

Hobbes smiled his thanks as Fergusen patted him on the shoulder and moved on. Hobbes's father, a street cop until his last breath, had checked out suddenly as he bought the morning paper on his way home from a multiple shift sixteen years before. He blew a tube—suffered a stroke—and died on the sidewalk where he'd spent his entire work life.

Hobbes wasn't yet twenty at the time, wrapped up in his pipe dreams as a playground and high school hoopster and dude about town, and going through an "I'm not you and I never will be" phase with his father. They didn't communicate. He thought his old man was a joyless stick.

Only on the day his father died did Hobbes begin to wake up to the things that eventually made him want to become the cop his father was.

The Robobots and the Tryptocons were vicious multiracial gangs that had overrun the working-class North End of the city where the Hobbes family lived. They were warring bloodily over the lucrative cocaine business that was just beginning to evolve into the insanity of the crack trade. Hobbes's father, though only a patrol sergeant, made up his mind they weren't going to destroy *his* precinct and neighborhood. He wasn't going to have his two boys grow up in a hellhole.

He set out quietly to chart every robbery, drug bust, shooting, mugging, gun report and felony warrant in his precinct. He made his men study the charts and go after the wolfpacks and gang-bangers where they were doing their work. He raided crack houses day after day until they shut down and moved to other precincts.

Hobbes learned at his old man's funeral that when he died he'd been up five days with almost no sleep on a round-the-clock surveillance/sting operation he was running. The aim was to roust out all the generals and foot soldiers of the two gangs, hassle them, bully them, chase them, threaten them, smear their reputations all over the North End. Almost singlehandedly and without fanfare or warfare he kept his precinct crack-free.

The instant his father went down, Hobbes began to feel the acute need for people like him in the world: hard-ass, often angry, but adamant in duty, never letting it slide. Gone was the rock and the pillar. His mother, a nurse's aide, never remarried. Hobbes still woke up at night with the feeling he wasn't being half the man he needed to be to replace the beacon that went out with his father.

Hobbes looked around for Gracie and his beer, hoping that Lou had forgotten his mission to needle.

"Come on, you can tell me," Lou said, "true or no? They say you never take cream." Like a dog with a juicy bone. Couldn't let it go.

"I don't like cream," Hobbes said simply.

"That means no?" Lou said, pressing.

"Yeah," Hobbes said. "No."

" 'No' as in 'Never?' or 'No' as in you do it, but you don't wanna talk about it?"

"Never."

"*Hobbesy*," Lou said with mock outrage. "This is the big city. We got a *tradition* to uphold."

"What's a matter, your ears don't work?" Jonesy said. "The man says something, he says it."

Hobbes spoke calmly, unemotionally, hoping to defuse Lou's pique. "I have a bed, roof, car," he said. "When I'm hungry, I eat. I meet a nice girl, I can afford to take her out. What else do I need?"

"A life," Lou said sarcastically. "So. Hypothetical: Other cops, who have families—"

Jonesy tried to run interference again. "Hobbes has a family, sort of—"

Lou pushed past him. "Other cops, who do feel the need to skim once in a while," Lou said, "a little something on the side—?"

"I don't judge," Hobbes said, again blandly, refusing to rise to the bait.

"You don't judge," Lou said, shaking his head. To Jonesy under his breath, "He's a fuckin' saint."

Hobbes tried to just ignore him.

"Are you tellin' me," Lou said intently to Hobbes, "under no circumstances would a holy man like you ever, you know, break the fuckin' law, do somethin' . . . ?"

Hobbes was tired of the game. He looked at Lou and said quietly, strongly: "Lou. I wanted to, I could reach over there and rip out your heart with my bare hands and squeeze the blood out and stuff it in your shirt pocket. If I lost control. But if I did, I'd be no different from the people we bust." He let that sink in a few seconds. "As to your general question about cops and cream"—he was a little uncomfortable spouting this out loud to another cop—"take anybody on the force, cream or no, ninety-nine percent of the time they're still doing their job, right?"

"Ninety-nine five," Jonesy said.

"Yeah, point five," Hobbes said. "So he, or she"—he glanced toward where Tiffany had sat—"is still doing more good every day than any lawyer, stockbroker or U.S. president does in a lifetime."

Lou stared at Hobbes. He *really* didn't expect this last opinion. Let alone what Hobbes said next.

"Cops are the chosen people," Hobbes said in his quiet, understated way.

Lou stared at him. It was hard to tell which way he was going to go on this. Finally he said, "Guess I'm switching to Bud." He laughed uproariously. Hobbes was okay. Lou grabbed the passing waitress. "Hey, Gracie, bring me three Buds, huh?—How 'bout you, Jonesy? Wanna go American?—And get this foreign shit off my table."

Hobbes and Jonesy both gave a good laugh. The tension was broken. Gracie shook her head and cleared some bottles: Fuckin' Lou. What gets into the guy?

CHAPTER 10

Hobbes, Jonesy and Lou left the bar. It was damned late, after three. Lou pulled his heavy parka around him, saluted and peeled off up the street to look for his car.

Hobbes and Jonesy walked in the other direction. They crossed the empty street and unlocked their cars.

"Boy, is he an asshole," Jonesy said.

"Yeah. Well," Hobbes said, "if there were no assholes, we wouldn't know what shit was."

Jonesy nodded. They parted, got in their cars and split off toward their homes.

And if there were no creeps and sadists and sickos, I wouldn't have a job, Hobbes thought as he drove, getting into one of those conversations with himself he tried his best to avoid. Evil crawled the earth, it was everywhere, maybe more widespread than good. How could that be if there was a Maker up there? Why would a Creator populate the human race with monsters? Plant evil seeds in all our hearts at one time or another? Made no sense. Unless maybe it was here as part of a larger plan: evil by its very existence pointing us toward what good was. Giving us the chance to choose to fight it and create a world just a little bit better than the one we found.

Oh, bullshit, he thought. All such religious-sound-

ing blather was a pile of rationalizations designed to
make him feel okay about what he'd done: Put a
man away, take away another man's right to live.

Get used to it, he told himself.

Reese had done it to himself by showing utter contempt for the lives of the people he tortured and
killed.

Sayonara.

Hobbes didn't need to justify his own actions by
inventing some cosmology in which he inhabited a
righteous place. They paid him to root out the sordid
human facts and track down murderers; they didn't
pay him to feel either good or bad about it or to
understand where it all fit in the Big Picture.

Hobbes's father had been a little-picture guy by
temperament and had drummed it into his two boys.
Take care of your front stoop and leave the grand
whys and wherefores to the pointy heads in ivory
towers. Guilt and breast-beating were for women and
poets, he'd say: "You're a cop, you're a grown-up.
You do what needs doing."

When Hobbes got home to his apartment he gave
himself the hammer blow of another stiff drink to
stop his mind from eating him alive and went
straight to bed. He fought off queasy images of Reese
singing and clowning behind his eyelids for three-
quarters of an hour, then fell asleep and slept the
sleep of the just.

CHAPTER 11

Hobbes slept the sleep of the just for what seemed about two minutes. The phone rang. He startled awake, his heart pounding. He looked at the glowing red numerals of the clock. 5:05 A.M. *Jesus.*

Groggy, he shook his head and reached for the phone. " 'Lo?" he said.

Silence on the other end.

"Hello?" he said sharply.

Nothing. Hobbes grabbed the telephone base and swung it around and looked at the "Caller ID" window. The window read: CALLER BLOCKED.

Hobbes frowned and muttered to himself: "Oh no. . . . Hello?" he said one more time.

Still no response.

He hung up, took the receiver off the hook and set it next to his beeper. He unplugged the receiver cord so no sound would emit. He was behaving as though the call was not simply a wrong number, not an isolated incident. Maybe it was, maybe it wasn't. Maybe it had nothing to do with the string of other middle-of-the-night calls he'd been getting the last few years. Logically, it couldn't be related. Still, he was in no shape to find out.

He took a drink of water and shook his head again. Still in a daze. But he was awake now, and feeling a low buzzing anxiety. He climbed out of bed in his T-shirt and boxers.

He padded down the hall. The door into the next bedroom was open, and a small night-light shined inside.

Hobbes pushed the door farther open and looked in.

Enough light to see the two beds, a single and a double. The bedclothes on the single were rumpled and pulled back; it had been slept in, but was empty. In the double were Hobbes's brother, Art, and Art's son, Sam, eight, curled up together.

Sweetest thing you ever saw.

Hobbes plodded out through the living room and checked the front door. Wandered into the kitchen, opened the refrigerator, stared distractedly at the white-lighted interior; gave up.

Checked the front door again, and the fire-escape window, and the windows along the hall. Trudged back to bed.

He lay awake for another three-quarters of an hour, trying not to relive Reese's last few minutes on earth.

What was to fear, really? The deed was done, the course was run. A man with a clean conscience. Sleep should have come easily.

And yet the scariest things are the simplest things, let's face it. A word, a sound, a look.

Silence.

Silence in the darkness.

CHAPTER 12

Rise and shine had come as soon as Hobbes closed his eyes, it felt like.

A bright Indian summer sun streamed in the grime-streaked kitchen windows, but Hobbes didn't notice. He dragged around trying to wake himself up and get some food into everybody.

Sam, the live wire, was devouring his cereal. Sam was a great-looking kid, slim, big brown eyes, good moves. He was cool, and he knew it, and he expected everybody else to know it, too.

Hobbes sat down with him to drink his coffee. A small TV was on, sound off. The news: images of Reese.

Art, the younger of the two Hobbes brothers, was at the counter, proudly packing Sam's lunch. Art in his favorite slouchy brown-checked bathrobe and slippers. He was more scholarly-looking than Hobbes, with big wire-framed glasses, a little stockier. Wide-eyed with a big ready smile.

"Here we go," Art said. "Milk, pretzels, apple, peanut butter and jelly sandwich—"

Sam's eyes immediately rolled, and he said under his breath to Hobbes, "Peanut butter and jelly sandwich. Uncle John, will you *please* make my lunch tomorrow?" Hobbes nodded as Sam went on in muted exasperation: "I can't eat the same thing every—"

A bicycle horn honked repeatedly outside the building. Art looked out the window and saw a lanky, floppy-haired boy about Sam's age circling on his bike, waving.

"T-h-e-r-e's . . . Toby!" Art said. He said it almost every morning, and with the same childish enthusiasm. Art, sweet-natured, willing man with those owlish specs and trim beard that made him look intellectual, was in fact mentally impaired.

Sam leapt up from the table, grabbed a bulging backpack and the sack lunch and gave his father a big hug, the irritation of a moment ago totally forgotten.

"I love you, Dad," Sam said cheerfully, heading toward his bike standing by the front door.

"Wait, wait," Art said, "don't forget—"

Sam tore back toward the table, and Hobbes just had time to half rise as Sam leapt into his arms. Hobbes caught him. Sam gave him a tight bear hug. Anyone witnessing the scene would know: Hobbes was the second parent here.

Sam jumped down, sprinted to his bike and wheeled it out the door, which Art was holding open. Art called after him, part of the ritual: "Have a good day at school!"

Art closed the door and shook his head. The joy was undiminished, no matter the mental capacity.

"What a kid," Hobbes said. "Come here, Art." He patted the chair next to him. "Have breakfast with me."

"You're not in a hurry or something?" Art said.

Hobbes looked out the window and watched Toby and Sam biking away. "Reese is dead," he said, "so I can relax, go in late for once."

Art was pleased. He rarely had time alone with Hobbes. Art came to the table, readied his breakfast and spoke shyly. "I love you, Johnny," he said.

Hobbes smiled wistfully. It was almost painful that his brother could hit this simple emotional level so naturally, gracefully.

"You ever think it would be easier," Art said, "your life would be so much easier or something, if Sam and I—"

"Stop," Hobbes said.

"Maybe Marcy wouldn't have left . . . if . . ."

"Art," Hobbes said. "Marcy was a jerk for leaving me. You're my brother. Sit down, huh?"

Art sat dutifully.

"I love you, too," Hobbes said.

Art smiled, brighter than any sunrise. He reached for the cornflakes.

It hadn't been easy for Art. A car hit him when he was twenty-five and left him the way he was now. A year after that, Julie, his wife and Sam's mother, had run out, unable to handle the strain of a changed, dependent husband. She left him Sam. Her letter said she knew how desperately he loved the boy, it was the least she could do. She went to Miami, where she was working as a singer-waitress in a hotel lounge, last they'd heard.

Hobbes took Art and Sam in the day she left.

And, yes, it did put added pressure on Hobbes's marriage. But the deformation and disintegration were already well under way. Marcy was out of there before a year was up. Art and Sam were just an excuse.

Hobbes's all-hours police work, the constant danger, the moods he brought home, the horror stories—those were the real causes. It took a peculiar kind of woman. Marcy just wanted a nonsordid life, a green lawn, no sirens, no listening with fear to names on the news night after night. Who could blame her?

Hobbes was thinking about Marcy, about the choices people make in their lives and how they learn who they are by making them.

He had chosen to pursue and marry Marcy. Why? Her big brown intelligent eyes and funny laugh. Her gentleness with all living things. Her passion, her gift for making him feel like he was the center of the universe.

Those were good reasons then. Great reasons. What man would want to resist?

But what did those traits and allures tell him about what would come later?—about this woman's capacity for undying loyalty under highly adverse circumstances? For keeping up her spirits living on a cop's meager salary? For giving up her own dreams in favor of his obsession with his work?

It had been long enough now, Hobbes had enough distance: He could no longer honestly say he would not have made the same choice in her shoes. He knew he had turned out to be no bargain as a husband. Could he have done differently, knowing what he knew now? Could he, for instance, have chosen another line of work? He didn't think so.

But still he missed her.

Art finished pouring himself some cornflakes and put the box back in the middle of the table, neatly, next to the sugar bowl, just the way Johnny liked it. Johnny was his god and his comfort; he would do anything to please Johnny.

"I love you, too, Art," Hobbes said again. "But don't make the boy any more peanut butter and jelly sandwiches."

CHAPTER 13

The cornflakes box sat in roughly the same spot in the middle of the table.

But a different table. A scarred, formica-topped metal breakfast table in the center of a different kitchen.

Charles the anorexic sat eating cornflakes. Erect posture, slightly formal manner. He used his left hand. He ate purposefully, taking his time, as though he wanted to do the job right.

The night before he had been casually dressed, the cheap tan baggy shirt worn outside his pants. Now he was in a newly pressed brown suit and tie.

As though mocking his fastidious appearance, the apartment around him was squalid to begin with and in disarray to boot: books and newspapers strewn, furniture knocked over. As if it had recently been the scene of an enormous struggle.

On the wall beside Charles something was scrawled in magic marker.

Charles placed his spoon in the bowl.

He looked down. There were four—and only four—objects on the table: the box of cornflakes, a half-gallon milk carton, a sugar bowl and, next to it in the center, the bowl of half-eaten cereal.

He adjusted the angle of the cornflakes box, moved the milk carton slightly.

The four objects now formed an odd, distinctive configuration.

Charles pushed back from the table and walked down the hall into the bathroom. He carefully applied toothpaste to his toothbrush and started to brush left-handed. The technique he used was just as the dentist taught. Small circles along the gum line. The toothpaste foamed. The man's face was blank, watching himself in the mirror, doing a very thorough job on those teeth.

Behind him was a grimy window, the bathtub and something sticking out of the tub—

A man's foot.

Attached to the foot, a man's body. Unclothed. Eyes open, terrified; mouth twisted. The only blood, a small puncture mark on the arm. But no mistaking it: dead as a carp.

Charles gargled, and spit. He carefully rinsed his mouth, then rinsed the toothbrush and left the bathroom.

He walked back down the hall and picked his way across the littered living room to the front door.

He opened it and turned to examine the apartment like a professional finishing a job. Everything just as he wanted it.

He stepped out, carefully closing the door behind him.

CHAPTER 14

Hobbes's precinct was a tough one, Midtown North, the Five-nine. He hadn't asked for it, but he hadn't asked out of it either. If you're going to be a cop, be a cop, his father had always said, by way of acceptance of his own tough postings.

What underlay that simple statement was the credo Hobbes had made his own: You could wear your uniform and ride around the nice quiet suburbs in a black-and-white, making sure nobody tipped over garbage cans; or you could go where your presence might make a life-or-death difference: the swarming city neighborhoods where people beat their kids and killed each other over a ten-dollar bill if there weren't cops around to jump on them.

Hobbes had started as a sore-foot rookie working patrol on the streets of the Seven-one, then the Five-oh. When he passed the sergeant's exam, he was assigned to the high-crime Midtown North, where he became known on the street for "t and t"—tactics and tirelessness. On a burglary call, when other cops instinctively converged on the center of action, Hobbes would gravitate to the most likely getaway route and often be in position to make a quick collar. Or, he would get to the roof of the highest building on the block and be in a position to see the suspect scrambling to escape over rooftops or in alleys.

He'd made his mark swiftly, and by the time he made detective at the young age of twenty-eight, he knew *all* the usual suspects: the whores, pimps, dealers, users, wife abusers, appliance boosters, shysters, bail bondsmen, fences.

He was famous for the number of C.I.s he had—confidential informants. Every two-bit thief and junkie north of Congress Street wanted Hobbes as his uncle: He came through with dollars for them when he said he would, and he never beat on them, no matter how badly they fucked up.

Instead, his style was just to turn around and walk away in disgust. When that happened, the lowlifes knew they'd have to work extra hard and come up with some good, bankable "real" for him—as in "Gimme the real, no wind"—to get back on his good side. It was a technique that seemed to work only for Hobbes. It worked because he had an uncanny ear for distinguishing real from bullshit and because a C.I. right in the middle of a spiel would see nothing but Hobbes's back if his Geiger counter went off.

Hobbes drove into the precinct's fenced-in lot and parked his old black Plymouth between two cruisers.

He headed toward the side door. He was getting in late this morning. Around 10 A.M.—bankers' hours. A self-indulgence that was actually pointless, since the more leisurely he was, the more the ghost of Reese danced in his mind. Only intense involvement in work and the passage of time would chase the creep away.

From a distance someone watched Hobbes.

Watched him drive in and park his car. Watched him get out, lock, walk toward the precinct. The

someone noted the time and twirled a fat cigar like
a self-satisfied mafioso. A mafioso in brown suit
and tie.

Just before he pulled the side door open, Hobbes
turned around and looked. He didn't see anything.
Something just told him to look.

He turned the knob and went in.

*One thing I believe is that we all know everything.
People know—not quite consciously—when something bad
is happening. When they're being watched, stalked.*

*Cops? A cop knows. A cop sees. Even the most casual
thing—it registers.*

*Sometimes you don't remember till later. You look back
and you realize: you knew.*

Charles the anorexic in his pressed brown suit,
standing across the street near the phone kiosk,
watching.

He took a little puff of his stogie. He had a look
like things were going just crackerjack.

He checked his watch again and leaned back
against the phone kiosk to wait.

CHAPTER 15

It was a squad room like every other one Hobbes had worked in. Practically out of the nineteenth century. Battered wooden desks covered with the lawman's nightmare—paperwork. File cabinets tall and small, all over the room, crammed with miscreant info, gang-banger info, spousal abuse info; waiting for the computer age to catch up and microfiche the mess.

A big chart on one wall detailing gang membership and hierarchy in the area of the precinct. A bulletin board with Stairmaster and Nordic Track and other mostly sports items listed on For Sale signs. Along with newspaper stories mentioning the precinct or the heroics of its members.

Hobbes was filling out some reports. His desk was remarkably clean for a working cop. Only a few objects, carefully, almost geometrically, placed; an accountant's desk.

Jonesy's littered desk was on one side of Hobbes. He was also working on reports. On the other side Tiffany was listening to a secretary-type sitting in the "guest chair"—the seat where complainants, witnesses, suspected perps sit and spill their beans.

Tiffany's guest was a thirty-three-year-old real estate pool secretary with spectacular nails and hair in

the once-again in bouff style. She was there to file.
On her live-in.

"He threatens me? Fine," she said. "He hits me?
I can deal. But how can you tell, Officer? If one day,
no warning, he's gonna really do it?" She looked
scared.

Tiffany was taking her dead seriously. But despair-
ing: Here was another of those "quivering on the
brink but no crime yet" cases. All Tiff would be able
to do was tell her where to go for an "order of pro-
tection," refer her to an abused women's shelter and
send her home. It broke her heart. Every time.

Hobbes looked at the woman, pondering her question, as his phone rang. Quick draw: "John Hobbes,"
he said, flat.

"Hey, pal, got a pen?" said a voice on the phone.
It was Charles the anorexic's voice.

"Who's this?" Hobbes asked.

"4541 South Stender, apartment 12C," the voice of
Charles said.

Hobbes jotted it down, bored. What was the beef
this time? A neighbor's kid urinating in the hall? The
superintendent was listening through the drains?

"What's there?" Hobbes said, hoping for something new, at least.

"A clue, Magoo," Charles said.

The line went dead. Hobbes hung up the phone,
considering the potential worth of the call.

Then he remembered. He turned to Jonesy.
"Couldn't sleep last night."

"Who can?" Jonesy said.

"Remember Reese used to call two, three a.m.?"
Hobbes said.

"He loved you, Hobbes, he truly did," Jonesy said
deadpan, pulling his chain. "That kind of devotion—"

"I had another call last night," Hobbes said.

Jonesy raised an eyebrow, interested.

Hobbes flicked the piece of paper with the address. He called across the room: "Yo, Denise, send a car to 4541 South Stender, huh?"

Denise, the efficient, neatly coiffed civilian clerk who answered the phone in the squad room, came over and got the paper from Hobbes.

"12C," Hobbes said. "Make sure we gain entry."

"DOA?" Denise asked. They got their fair share of those. The police were the first call neighbors made when they smelled a funny smell coming from inside a locked apartment.

"I doubt it," Hobbes said. "Probably some bozo saw my name in the paper, wants to impress his girl."

"Maybe saw you on TV," Jonesy said, wiggling his eyebrows.

"How'd I look, by the way?" Hobbes said with a grin. "I was on four channels." Held up four fingers.

Jonesy rolled his eyes.

Denise went off with the slip of paper.

Hobbes returned to his report writing.

Tears began to run down the cheeks of the pool secretary with big hair as she admitted to Tiffany she was terrified to go home, but had nowhere else to go.

CHAPTER 16

An unmarked police car pulled up to 4541 South Stender. It was a neighborhood where the city was slow to fix potholes in the street and the pawn shop was one of the most upscale and bustling businesses. An egg roll joint, a nail parlor, a Haitian spice shop and a tattoo studio faced the row of rundown apartments where 4541 was located.

4541 was a brownstone built when Coolidge was president, and it was still awaiting its first renovation. Bars on the ground-floor windows were the only updated touch.

A few people on the street rubbernecked at the collection of half a dozen police cars out front, but they went their way, not even bothering to ask what was going on. They already knew. Another crack murder, another overdose, a knifing in a stairwell. Life went on as usual. Just stay out of my building.

Hobbes and Jonesy got out of the unmarked car and made their way toward the brownstone.

They'd gotten the call from the black-and-white sent over by Denise. Record time. About twelve minutes and the beat cops were back on the phone to the precinct: bingo. You win a kewpie doll, Detective Hobbes. Get over here and collect.

Hobbes knew the neighborhood. He pointed down

the street at the coin laundry on the corner. They'd
picked the body of a newborn baby out of a laundry
hamper there two years ago.

Jonesy looked; he remembered. Baby dressed in
gown and bonnet and laid to rest on towels. They
never found the mother.

They hurried inside 4541.

The bathroom was a popular place. A prints technician dusted the chrome fixtures while another one
picked hairs off the towel hanging on the rack and
put them in a Ziploc sandwich bag.

A guy from the medical examiner's office stood by
with his latex gloves on, holding a thermometer with
a nine-inch probe, waiting to stick it into the de-
ceased's liver. Liver temperature matched to a text-
book forensic chart would determine the time of
death within a quarter of an hour, assuming the guy
had departed within the last forty-eight.

Flash.

Jonesy took a Polaroid of the face of the body in
the bathtub. Another from below the feet. Another
including the wall with the grimy window as background. Maybe later the pix would reveal details
they were overlooking now.

A big-faced uniformed cop told Jonesy and Hobbes
what he'd found out. "Name's Muskavich," he said.
"Russian expatriate. Super says no family, no friends,
no nothin'."

"Then why's he dead?" Hobbes said.

Jonesy and the big-faced cop laughed.

"Whattaya see?" Hobbes asked Jonesy.

Jonesy now had his own disposable latex gloves
on and was examining the body. "No visible
wounds," he said. "Except three puncture marks.

Here, here and here." Shoulder, arm, neck. "Look around for a syringe or something," he said to the big-faced cop.

He moved up and took another Polaroid. He pointed Hobbes to the number 18 in magic marker on the man's chest. "What's this, it's his eighteenth victim?"

"I guess," Hobbes said, drifting out of the bathroom. "We better check the MO."

Jonesy followed him out into the living room. The rest of the apartment remained exactly as the first cops had found it. A baby-faced cop guarded the door. Clothes lay heaped on the floor.

Hobbes and Jonesy walked into the kitchen area and checked out the breakfast table. The breakfast stuff was just as the last occupant had left it: the odd configuration of four objects. Neat. Purposefully arranged.

"Looks like your desk," Jonesy said, joking.

"The DOA's been dead a while, so what's this?" Hobbes said. "The killer slept over? Ate a nice breakfast?"

Jonesy checked the used bowl, spoon. "Seems like," he said. He straightened up, looked around. And saw something behind the door. He pulled the door out of the way. "Hey, check it out," he said. He was looking at the magic-marker writing on the wall.

Hobbes turned. Stared.

His blood ran cold as ice.

Written on the wall in a cursive crawl.

> *Lyons*
> *???*
> *Spakowsky*

Hobbes continued to stare.

Jonesy noticed the intensity. "What?" he said.

Hobbes shook his head, finally found what was left of his voice. "A riddle," he said. "Something Reese asked."

"Say it again?" Jonesy said.

"In his cell before he died," Hobbes said, "Reese asked me: 'Why is there a space between Lyons and Spakowsky?'"

Flash.

Jonesy took a Polaroid of the message on the wall. And stood staring at it, hard put to come up with a good explanation. How could Reese's peculiar private exchange with Hobbes show up on the wall here?

There was of course a simple explanation. But until he heard it, he was going to have to live with the sudden, uneasy feeling he had at that moment.

Hobbes stood there, taking deep breaths, sorting through explanations in his mind. Fucking Reese. Fucking Reese and his mind games. Reaching beyond death to somehow kill and then rub Hobbes's nose in it. Thank God he was one of a kind. Thank God he was in the grave. He was a creature with a genius for torment, and the world was well rid of him.

CHAPTER 17

Lieutenant Stanton wasn't tickled at what he saw as he stood at Hobbes's desk. He was looking at the Polaroids of the writing from Muskavich's wall. He lowered the pictures and shook his head. "Reese had an accomplice?" he said with disgust.

"Or else it's copy-cat," Hobbes said. "The guard at the prison, the guys making the film."

Stanton nodded. "Fifty people coulda seen that film by now."

"Swell," Hobbes said. "So Jonesy and I'll run 'em down."

Jonesy gave him silent finger from where he sat at his desk.

Stanton smiled, he had been there. Legwork. The dirty little secret behind the glamor job of detective. It seemed like every case demanded more than the last.

Detective Lawrence came up to him. "You got a minute?" he asked. The wiry Lawrence with his sharp street clothes looked more like a made man than usual.

"Sure," Stanton said, and went with him.

Jonesy hung up the phone, turned to Hobbes. "Fingerprint," he said. "The perp didn't wear gloves.

Left prints on the spoon, cereal bowl: like he's advertising."

"Must be his prints aren't in the system," Hobbes said. "Still—kinda like waving red flags at us. The phone call included."

Jonesy nodded agreement.

Lou looked up from his desk ten feet away. "I hate to be stupid, huh—?" he started to say.

"Enjoy it, Lou—" Jonesy said, ready to cut off Lou's crude attempts at sarcasm at the knees.

Lou flashed him a fuck-you glare. Jonesy was on Lou's case because of the lip Lou gave Hobbes in the bar.

Lou had something to say, though, and he was going to say it. "But is motive still something we should think about," he said, "or are all crimes done for their own sake, outta sickness?"

Tiffany heard that as she walked by. She mimed hitting a buzzer: "Bzzzz. Number two."

Jonesy came back to Lou in his offhand but typically astute manner. "Everything has motive," he said. "Sickness is motive, too."

This thought hovered for a moment.

In the background Denise was distributing burritos. Lou picked up pages from the fax machine: a page for him, something for Hobbes and Jonesy. He nosily read theirs on his way over to drop them off.

"Look sharp, Bud," he said, handing Hobbes his fax. Hobbes was "Bud" for now, thanks to his choice of beers. "Coroner's prelim on the Rooskey," Lou announced. "Isn't this that wacko poison Reese used on those Arab kids?"

Hobbes examined the fax with concern. Lou was right.

Denise reached Hobbes's desk with the burritos order. "Chicken, spicy with onions?" she said, holding out a package.

Hobbes looked up at Denise. He knew she'd said something to him, but had no idea what. He nodded absentmindedly.

"Hey, Lawrence," he said. "You're hip, right?"

Lawrence looked at him, raising a brow. Sounded like a setup. "I have my moments," he said warily.

"Tell me this," Hobbes said. "Why is there a space between Lyons and Spakowsky?"

Lawrence stared blankly. "That's a hip question?" he said. "To me, that is not a hip question."

Hobbes looked around. Everyone had stopped eating their burritos. "Tiff, you like puzzles and shit, brainteasers?" he said.

"Long as I'm doing the teasing," she said, chewing her gum and grinning.

"Why is there a space between Lyons and Spakowsky?" he said.

Tiffany frowned, shook her head. "What's that even mean, man?"

Hobbes shook his head: He didn't know.

A lingering beat. People started to munch on their burritos again.

Lou shrugged, spoke with his mouth full: "We had a Spakowsky my rookie year. South River precinct?" He shook his head as though to say, What an asshole.

Hobbes turned toward Lou, who was chomping away on his third burrito already.

"Come again?" Hobbes said.

Lou waved him off. "Not *your* Spakowsky," he said. "This guy was a cop."

"Keep talking, Lou," Hobbes said.

"Man, he was the King Kong of assholes," Lou said. "I'm talking legend, huh? His name is on the fuckin' wall."

Hobbes blinked.

CHAPTER 18

The Five-nine Precinct basement held the showers and lockers, as well as the evidence lockup, the supplies and storage area and the records room, such as it was. The records room was in the back of the cellar, behind a chain-link fence and locked gate.

Lou led Hobbes down the dingy basement hall and unlocked the gate. Inside were row on row of cardboard boxes filled with old case folders, metal cabinets with personnel files and miscellaneous junk going back fifty years. It was poorly lit. Spooky down there. The kind of shadowy basement where it was easy to let the imagination run wild and see strange things lurking in the dark corners.

Hobbes himself probably had the most boxes of case files down there, including one whole box for each of the death penalty cases he'd had, seven previous to Reese. Those files included pleadings and depositions from the dozens and dozens of appeals the cases had gone through. In none of those cases was there even the shred of a possibility that he'd got the wrong man, Hobbes was sure. He'd reviewed and personally investigated every bit of "new evidence" the lawyers brought up on appeal until he was confident no miscarriage of justice was being perpetrated. Only after the man had been executed had his box of case files gone to the basement.

"Spozedly some chief in the thirties thought it'd boost morale," Lou said, pulling the chain on an overhead lightbulb to illuminate one such corner. "They kept with it till like '81 or so." He pulled some boxes out of the way. "It got like a booby prize."

He exposed a big rectangular metal commendation plaque leaning against the wall. Three feet by four feet. It had an ornate crest and the words in bronze:

FOR OUTSTANDING AND COURAGEOUS VALOR

"Remember?" Lou said. "It was downtown till they went with the remodel." He ran a flashlight down the edges of the plaque where bronze name plates were soldered. Names for consecutive years decade after decade.

Lou stopped when he got to 1964. The name plate read:

1964—GEORGE LYONS

The slot below—for 1965—was empty, just knots of old solder remaining where a name plate had been removed. The name plate below that read:

1966—ANTON SPAKOWSKY

Lou shrugged. "You musta passed it a thousand times," he said.

"Yeah," Hobbes said. He quoted what he remembered Reese saying: "I just had to 'open my eyes, look around sometime.' "

"Lyons musta retired by my time," Lou said. "But Spakowsky, he was still around—"

"Lou—?" Hobbes said.

"He was so mean," Lou went on, ignoring Hobbes, on a riff, "his wife finally shot him in a foot. Son of a bitch couldn't get disability—"

"Lou," Hobbes said again. "Why is there a space here? Who was '65?"

Lou stared at the plaque, the missing name plate. He shrugged. "You got me, bud."

They both stared in silence.

Hobbes slowly realized how aggravated he was. *"Why is there a space between Lyons and Spakowsky?"* Reese had said to him in his death row cell. By then—how else to explain it?—Reese had already arranged for somebody to murder Muskavich, or maybe any random victim, and scribble this riddle on the wall of the murdered person's apartment. Was it all just to torment Hobbes? Would anybody really go so far to exact this weird psychological revenge?

Only a madman.

But putting it down to insanity didn't make it any easier to swallow. That only meant he was dancing like a marionette on the strings of a madman.

In the squad room Stanton stood by the table in the coffee area, adding milk to his java. Hobbes was pouring some mud for himself.

"They took a name off?" Stanton said, frowning. "Why would they do that?"

"I called Records," Hobbes said. "They say they don't know who it was, don't know why it's not there."

"Well. We better find out, huh?" Stanton said, showing some irritation at Records, and walking away.

Hobbes nodded at Stanton's back, watching him go. Curious, he thought. Stanton could have offered to pick up the phone and make a couple of calls downtown. He could have easily found out the missing name for him and why it had been taken off. If in fact it had been removed and not just accidentally knocked off when the plaque was retired.

Stanton wasn't too interested apparently.

Stanton must not have cottoned onto exactly what was going on here, Hobbes thought with anger. Then he brought himself up short.

He *was* dancing like a puppet on a string. Reacting exactly as Reese had hoped, no doubt. Overreacting. He had to cool out, figure this thing out rationally and put it behind him.

CHAPTER 19

Hobbes's apartment was quiet, dark and still. Art and Sam slept in their bedroom. A muted clicking coming from behind a closed door. Hobbes's bedroom.

From the street a watcher would have seen it was the only lighted room in that corner of the building.

Hobbes sat at his desk in his bedroom. The few objects on the surface were arrayed tidily, as on his desk at the precinct. Computer in the middle, address book with its corners aligned with the desk's corners. Pens and pad at a precise forty-five-degree angle.

That's the kind of mind Hobbes had: He liked imposing organization on the anarchic reality around him. Only when he could do that was he comfortable. It was a mental trait he'd no doubt inherited from his bookkeeper grandfather—the neat rows of figures that all added up, the double-entry accounting that reconciled at the end of every month. A little corner of order in a world of random bedlam.

It was what he did as a police detective: lined up the elements of means, motive and opportunity to make a case; amassed fact upon fact until all the facts added up to coherent explanations of the human messes he was called in on.

It was the middle of the night, and he knew it was

pointless to try to sleep. He was on his computer, on-line, going through many-years-old issues of the daily paper. Back to the sixties.

He found a front-page article that gave him a start at what he was after. It had a photograph of George Lyons and a headline: LYONS DECORATED FOR 1964.

He looked at the top of the page, the date: *February 12, 1965.*

He pressed SEARCH and typed in *February 12, 1966.* The year after, the year of the missing plaque.

The 1966 front page for February 12 popped up. He scanned it: nothing.

He hit two keys and got the front page for the day before, February 11. He skimmed that one: nothing.

He tried more front pages in either direction, without success. Kept at it . . .

Then he stopped. He moved closer to the screen and read. Below the fold, down in one corner, a headline: MILANO NAMED COP OF THE YEAR 1965. And the subhead read, "Detective nabbed 'Ivy League Killer.' "

The photograph showed a handsome dark-haired man with an honest face, in a blue uniform.

Hobbes pressed SEARCH and typed in "Robert Milano." The screen said "Searching . . ."

An article popped up about Milano making another arrest. Hobbes scanned it quickly, absorbed the details.

He hit SEARCH again on the name "Robert Milano." He waited . . . waited . . .

Something came up. He stared. The eerie computer light flickering over his face.

He sat back and tried to make the information on the screen fit somewhere in the Reese puzzle.

Not even close.

He hit PRINT.

He got up and paced in front of his window. Had he stopped and leaned close to the pane he might have seen him. But he didn't.

He went back to his desk and picked up the printed page from the printer. He read it again as he continued pacing.

Outside, across the street, a figure in a coat and tie and raincoat stood in the cold and watched the silhouette in the lighted window. The person watched closely, interestedly, as Hobbes moved slowly by the patch of light, tracked him as though monitoring his thoughts.

A skinny, smirking guy with an attitude. A guy who used to be relatively happy delivering sandwiches.

CHAPTER 20

Hobbes dragged into the precinct in the morning after a ratty four hours of sleep. He caught up with Stanton as he was walking toward his office and handed him the page he'd printed out last night.

"Off the Net," he said.

Stanton scanned down the article. "Robert Milano," he said.

"Yeah," Hobbes said. "Cop of the Year 1965. Eight months later, he goes to some cabin in the middle of nowhere and dies 'cleaning his gun.' So either it was a woman or he was dirty, right?"

Stanton gave Hobbes an unreadable look, handed him back the sheet and continued toward his office. "I met him once. Milano," he said. "He had a poker up his ass, but otherwise he was a good cop."

"Okay," Hobbes said with an impatient smile, "but what I want to know is—"

"I know what you want," Stanton said, cutting him off, "but I can't help you on this."

Hobbes was incredulous—and outraged. "You can't help me?"

"Just do us all a favor, huh?" Stanton said, low. "Whatever you find out, keep it to yourself."

A silent beat. They looked at each other.

"Okay," Hobbes said sarcastically. He didn't get

it, but if that's the way it was going to be: "See you at the annual picnic." He started to walk away.

"Hold on, I got somethin'," Stanton said. He held up a videotape. "Reese. That documentary thing they were shooting at the prison." He tossed it to Hobbes.

"Thanks, Stan," Hobbes said with a definite edge. "You're a white man."

He walked out of Stanton's office at a low boil. Politics. Had to be. One thing Hobbes couldn't abide was politics, shadowy, self-promoting, ass-protecting motives behind departmental dealings. It had taken him an extra year or two to make detective because he wouldn't play politics and kiss up to his sector commander at the time.

He walked across the squad room past Jonesy's desk. He held up the videotape: "Tape on Reese, wanna view?"

"Give me a sec," Jonesy said.

"How 'bout Muskavich," Hobbes said. "What's in?"

"Fingerprints are a bust," Jonesy said. "Crime Scene says"—he flipped through his notebook—"killer's probably dark-haired . . . also probably left-handed . . ."

Hobbes said, idly, giving it no significance, "Like Reese."

"Yeah. And his teeth are bad," Jonesy said.

Hobbes gave him a look.

"Found a piece in the cornflakes," Jonesy said, heading off for the Xerox machine.

Hobbes put down the tape. He looked at the print-out of the newspaper page still in his hand. He picked up the phone, dialed 411.

An operator's voice came on: "This is Debra, what listing?"

Hobbes scanned the clipping at the bottom where it said "Detective Milano is survived by his wife, Sylvia, 35, and daughter Gretta, 8 months old." He said into the phone, "Sylvia Milano. M-I-L-A-N-O."

Stanton was passing Hobbes's desk as he waited for the listing on the phone.

Hobbes leaned back and jabbed at him: "Hey, Lieutenant. If someone else dies 'cause you're keepin' your mouth shut, you're holding the bag, not me."

Stanton stopped in his tracks. Thought a second. "When it's a perfect world, Detective, lemme know, okay?" he said. "In the meantime: I am *not* the one who's keepin' his mouth shut. Is that clear enough for you?"

Hobbes thought about it as Stanton moved away. It was a little clearer, but not much. Still a big Why? hanging over the whole thing. A *big* Why. Thirty years the man'd been in the ground, and still there was something the department didn't want aired?

Up at the front of the squad room, Denise was handing Jonesy a memo.

Hobbes watched him reading it as the operator's voice came back on the phone. "I'm sorry," she said. "There's no such listing."

"Okay, thanks," Hobbes said, and started to hang up. Then another thought. "Wait," he said, "What about . . . You there?" He examined the clipping again. "Under Milano: Do you have a Gretta or an initial 'G'?"

Jonesy just then sauntered back to his desk opposite Hobbes's, waving the memo Denise had delivered to him. "The syringe with the poison," he said. "Has the same prints as the spoon and bowl." He shrugged. Dead end, not in the system. "So what now? Video time?"

Hobbes tossed him the videotape.

"You know," Jonesy said, "I been thinking—"

Lou jumped on that quick as a ferret. "Whoa, easy boy. Don't hurt yourself." He grinned his evil grin.

The operator spoke in Hobbes's ear. "Please hold for the number . . ."

Hobbes jotted down the number as Jonesy went on. "Whoever killed Muskavich," he said, "knows the poison Reese used. And he's quoting Reese. . . . It could be a cop."

Hobbes dialed Gretta Milano's number as he talked. "I've thought of that," he said. He looked over at Lou suggestively. "Could be a cop, huh, Lou?" he said jokingly.

Gretta Milano's voice came on the phone: "Hi. Please leave a message." . . . *Beep*—

"Ahh . . . this is Detective John Hobbes," he said smoothly. "Could you please call me? 555-9594. Thanks a lot."

He hung up the phone. He got up and led the way toward the video room, waving Jonesy on.

"What was that with your voice?" Jonesy said.

"How you mean?" Hobbes said as they threaded their way through the other desks toward a small storage room at one side that served as the video room.

"You made your voice go soft," Jonesy said. "What, it was a girl of something? She sounded cute?"

Hobbes playfully cuffed Jonesy. Caught. He covered it up. "I'll let you know after I see her, huh?"

CHAPTER 21

Reese on the TV screen was gesturing and singing, wild and raucous, "Time Is on My Side." It was his performance in the gas chamber after he was strapped in and the sweep hand was making the final revolution before the gas was released. His burst of song to go out on. The moment had enraged the governor and brought a begrudging smile to Hobbes's face.

Jonesy shook his head at the psycho's antics on the screen. "Used to have a lounge act," he said.

Hobbes rewound the tape.

"You don't wanna go to the end?" Jonesy said. "Make sure he's dead?"

"I wanna see the priest again," Hobbes said. He pressed PLAY. The tape ran. It was a scene in Reese's cell the filmmakers had recorded earlier in the day, before Hobbes's arrival.

A priest was talking to one of the death row guards, asking him to unlock Reese's cell door.

Reese could be heard muttering something off camera; the camera panned to him. As he came into the frame, Reese spoke in a clear, quiet and deadly voice: "Father," he said. "Step in here, I'll kill you."

"You don't really mean that," the priest was heard saying, off camera.

Reese gave a nasty half smile. "Five seconds," he said. That's all it would take.

The documentary camera quick-panned to the priest's face. Bemused alertness.

Pan to Reese: calm, motionless, homicidal.

The camera panned back to the priest, now hesitating. He looked at the guard, who shrugged.

The documentary maker panned back and forth on this primitive game of chicken. Reese staring. The priest staring back, trying to make a judgment.

Reese gestured casually with his hand: Come on in, dude.

The priest was still staring, and suddenly, from the look of his face, a chill crept into his bones. He blinked. Lost it.

He turned, spoke softly to the guard and walked away.

Reese screamed, "Coward!" He grabbed the bars, yelled after the priest, "How can you serve God if you ain't got any balls?!"

Then, eerily, his voice flat, he turned toward the camera and said, "Make sure Hobbes gets a copy of this, huh?"

His voice changed again. "Johnny boy," he said, "you watching?" He waved at the camera with a weird three-finger sign. "I hope you're paying close attention. Every gesture, every word . . ."

Abruptly, Reese shut down. It was a freaky sight: live to dead in two seconds. Eyes closed. Motionless. End of scene.

Hobbes froze the face and looked at it for a thoughtful moment or two. Then he fast-forwarded to where he himself came in. He started to go past it, but Jonesy spoke up.

"Hold a sec," he said. "I wanna . . ." He took the

remote, pressed PLAY, and it was Reese saying, "Open your eyes, pal. Look around—"

Jonesy pressed REVERSE, and the tape rewound.

He pressed PLAY again. Now it was back to Reese shaking Hobbes's hand, holding onto it—muttering, "Still a good boy." He tried to lift, rub and fondle Hobbes's hand; Hobbes yanked it back.

Jonesy let the tape run.

"Hey, I'm not your priest," Hobbes was saying.

Reese grinned harshly. "Sure you are," he said, then launched into a muttered dirge, nonsense syllables of some kind, fast and unintelligible, under his breath.

Offscreen, Hobbes could be heard saying, "I hope you're having fun."

At that, Reese wigged out, did his sudden weird pantomime. "Touched" the air, "fucked" his fist with his index finger, rubbed his palms together. Very peculiar.

Jonesy marveled at the guy: He had no quit in him. "You said later he was talking Dutch?" Jonesy said. "So this is Dutch, too?"

"This?" Hobbes said. "This is hocus-pocus mumbo jumbo."

"Oh," Jonesy said. "You sure on that?"

Hobbes blinked, wondering. With Reese you could never be sure of anything. His real agenda tended to be one or two levels removed from what it appeared to be.

CHAPTER 22

Hobbes's car rolled slowly through the university's residential neighborhood at twilight. Students with backpacks and bookbags walked along in groups and singly under the big old oaks and elms that hung over the streets. Many of them walked leisurely as though they were already in the place they wanted to be, not hurrying madly to get somewhere else. Pleasant surroundings, more pleasant than Hobbes could afford to live in. Much more pleasant than the environs where he spent most of his working days.

Hobbes, actually beginning to feel a bit relaxed for the first time since the execution, turned onto Comstock Street and started looking for the particular address.

The light was fading, the street lights came on. The night air was temperate. A pair of students crossed in front of his slowing car and gave him a smile on their way by.

This was another world, a normal world, far apart from the vengeful psychopaths and ghastly homicides of a police detective's existence. Ordinary people going about their benign business, playing out healthy desires and ambitions. The difference struck

Hobbes like an unexpected breeze with the scent of wildflowers.

On one side of Comstock was a park, on the other a row of Edwardian-Gothic mansions converted into apartments. Hobbes pulled over to the curb and turned off his engine. He sat back and trained his gaze on a particular building.

A woman came up the walk, carrying a briefcase, wearing a muted maroon scarf and gray herringbone overcoat. Proper and conservative. Pretty.

Hobbes checked his notebook. Gretta Milano would be thirty-two now, he figured from the newspaper.

The woman entered the building.

For some reason Hobbes didn't have a moment's doubt it was she. He got out of his car, crossed the street, sprinted up the steps and caught the outer door before it closed. He followed her in.

He took his time and let her get safely inside her apartment on the second floor. He climbed the stairs and rang her bell. Waited.

The viewing hole opened on the other side.

Silence. Just watching.

"My name is John Hobbes," he said. "I'm looking for Gretta Milano."

A longish beat, then the door opened.

Gretta looked him over. Her air was pleasant, noncommittal. She was beautiful in a glancing, ethereal sort of way. But grounded. It was the eyes: dark, unblinking, penetrating. "Yes, you called before," she said.

"Yeah," Hobbes said. "I want to talk to you about your father."

Her face changed slightly. Yet she did not let him in.

Hobbes held up his badge in his right hand. She
looked at his badge, then again at his face. First com-
paring them, then looking into his eyes. An assess-
ment. She seemed to be seeking to satisfy herself
about something, but said nothing.

Hobbes had never felt quite so "looked over" as
at that moment. It was the intensity in her gaze as
well as the gravity. What was she assessing?

Her look changed slightly. He sensed he somehow
had passed muster.

"May I come in?" he asked.

She nodded, opened the door for him and stood
back. As he entered, he could have sworn he saw a
kind of resignation and acceptance on her face, as
though she had been expecting him to come sooner
or later.

Gretta's apartment was an old-fashioned high-ceil-
inged place that gave a sense of air, space. The indi-
rect lighting gave the white walls an immateriality.
This effect was intensified by the art work: reproduc-
tions of Pre-Raphaelite angels. Small oils. Statuettes.
Friezes. Lots of angels. The impact was quite striking,
and Hobbes couldn't help commenting. "You're surrounded by angels," he said.

Gretta answered matter-of-factly, "I teach theology
at the U."

"They're beautiful," Hobbes heard himself saying.
What was getting into him—such charm? He knew
very well, looking at her. She *was* beautiful. Soft,
chin-length brown hair brushing her cheeks. And
those dark, liquid eyes that seemed to be looking
so searchingly.

"Why do you want to know about my father?"
Gretta said neutrally.

"Well, it's thirty years later," Hobbes said, "the

files are sealed and my boss is being told to let it alone."

He checked himself: What am I doing? he thought, laying it right out there like that. Not like him to be so unguarded with in-house info. And yet he felt strangely certain that in her case it was the right thing to do.

She had an ironic reaction to his statement. On the stove, her tea kettle whistled. She looked at him and decided to take the first step. She turned and headed for the kitchen. A signal for him to follow.

"Detective," she said as she turned the heat off under the kettle, "I could tell you what my mother told me before she died."

"I'm sorry—" he said, on the chance her death was recent.

Gretta held up a hand. "Please," she said. "But why do you want to know? Is it idle curiosity, or—"

"No," Hobbes said. "See, I'm the guy who caught Edgar Reese, who was just executed."

"Yes, I read about it," she said.

"Reese kind of . . . gave me your father's name," he said.

She looked at him blankly. Then, struck by a thought, she said, "Did Reese sing at the execution?"

"Well, actually he did," he said, surprised, "yes."

"And he touched you or grabbed you or . . . ?"

Hobbes felt the hair on his neck tingling. This was definitely spooky. "Shook my hand," he said. "How did you know that?"

She absorbed that without answering. But her manner changed, her voice changed. As though she'd made yet another decision about something and was going to act on it. "You want some coffee?" she said, reaching into the cupboard for another cup.

"Please," Hobbes said.

Gretta talked as she poured water from the kettle over some filters. "One condition," she said. "You and I never spoke. You say nothing to your partner, your boss. Nothing goes in the files. My name, and everything I say, is just between us. Is that agreeable?"

"All that for a cup of coffee?" he said, smiling.

She half smiled. Gave him his cup.

They both stirred.

"In 1965," she said, "there was a police corruption scandal. In '66 my father was decorated, pride of the force and all that. A short time after, he shot himself."

Hobbes nodded. "Cleaning his gun."

"Yeah, right," she said. "Two years later a reporter found out Dad had been under investigation. He'd caught a killer, but copycat crimes were occurring. Evidence was mounting: witnesses, fingerprints. The press never got real proof, but my father's medal was rescinded."

Hobbes wasn't surprised by any of this. "You're saying . . . when he died: Somebody made this evidence go away?"

She nodded slightly.

He muttered, "That's a felony."

Gretta nodded again. "The mayor, governor, chief of police," she said. "They all needed a hero. Some of these people are still important."

"I see," he said.

"Not yet, you don't," she said. "My father saw the evidence against him. He told my mother he had no chance to beat it. So he went up to a cabin in the mountains, a place that's been in my mother's family sixty years. He went there and . . ." Well, she knew he knew the rest of the story.

At that instant he felt with a certainty he knew what had actually happened—a picture of events that probably she didn't have. A deal, is what Hobbes was thinking. The brass offered Milano a deal: Blow your brains out, and we'll protect your name, your family, your death benefits. This was not a conjecture he intended to lay on the dead man's daughter.

Gretta frowned with the memories. "The thing is, Detective," she went on, "I know . . . for a fact . . . that my father was innocent of those murders."

"How do you know?" Hobbes said.

She looked at him unblinking, again assessing.

"How do you know he was innocent?" he said again.

She stared at him. "It's thirty years ago," she said. "It's not important anymore."

An evasion like that said she was keeping volumes of information from him. "It's important to me," he said. "If you're saying someone else did it and the killer's still alive . . ."

A hint of an ironic smile flashed across her face.

"There's no statute of limitations on murder," he said.

"I'm aware of that," she said.

"So don't you want the truth to come out?" he said. "Don't you want the killer punished?"

"Of course . . ."

Hobbes started to get the drift. "But . . . what?" he said. "You're afraid if you tell me, you'll be in danger."

"Well . . . kind of," she said. "Yes."

They looked at each other. Hobbes waited. Finally: "That's it?"

She nodded.

He felt absolutely certain that wasn't it. There was much more behind her reticence than she was telling him. But the way she put it amounted to erecting a wall; he couldn't very well poo-poo her fear. Who knew? She could very well be right about the danger.

He stood up and moved toward the door.

"Okay, thanks for the coffee," he said. "If I have further questions, can I—"

She hesitated, then politely said, "I'd really rather you didn't."

He nodded. He was thrown by her blunt insistence on cutting off further contact. Her father, in her eyes, had been a victim of a miscarriage of justice; Hobbes was offering to dig at it, maybe rectify it. No matter. She wasn't giving him that choice. She was giving him the boot, closing the door on him.

He went into her front hall and opened the door. He nodded his thanks and walked out, closing the door behind him.

She had a last thought and quickly opened the door. "Do you believe in God, Mr. Hobbes?" she asked as he was starting down the stairs.

Now, that threw him slightly. She was capable of surprising him at every turn, it seemed.

"Yeah. I go to church now and then," he said. "In my job, seeing what I see, faith is kind of hard to sustain."

She held the door open and looked him in the eye. "What you see in your job is nothing," she said. And, quickly and softly, before she closed the door, "Good luck." And she was gone.

Whoa, Hobbes thought, staring at the door. What a chilling thing to say. Hobbes turned and started down the stairs.

CHAPTER 23

Hobbes parked his car, got out, and walked up the street through the crisp night air toward his apartment.

He lived in Uptown, the same middle- to low-income section of the city in which he worked. That was the right place for a cop to live, he felt.

His street, neither fancy nor shabby, was full of middle-class apartment houses where Eastern European and Asian immigrants were just as comfortable as fourth-generation Irish and African Americans. Window boxes with pansies. Swept sidewalks. No trash in the gutter. A place where Hobbes could help his brother raise his son and feel relatively safe. Though Hobbes knew, if fate took a hankering for you, nowhere was really safe.

He had left Gretta's with his mind doing somersaults. Far from departing with answers, he'd walked away with more puzzles. Reese, for example. She somehow knew about Reese's singing, his touching. What the hell?

The ride home hadn't helped his frame of mind. And now, walking the half block from his car to his building, he was still twisting his brain into a snarl. He passed a few other pedestrians without even no-

ticing them. Not many walkers on the street just then,
but a few.

*Sometimes I think the basic job human beings have is
to figure out what the hell is going on.*

A man was strolling up the street toward Hobbes.
Taking his time, enjoying the foliage in the overhang-
ing trees, breathing the fresh evening air. An unex-
ceptional-looking man in a bluish leather coat. With
a kind of arrogant half smile. Thin.

*Take this thing with Gretta Milano. Of course I wanted
to know what she was hiding. What was she scared of?
Why she ended things so abruptly.*
*And her final questions, about God, what was that
about?*

The strolling man reached Hobbes. Charles the anorexic. Only lately an ill-dressed, slow-witted, slow-
footed delivery man. Now a leather-coated citizen
with a confident gait and purposeful look about him.

As he passed, he looked Hobbes in the eye. Hobbes
looked back.

For an instant their eyes locked.

Charles's face betrayed the hint of a mocking smile
as they passed each other.

Hobbes took sudden note of that look, that smile. A
vague apprehension skated across his consciousness.

Both men kept walking, neither one turning or
breaking stride.

You never know. Down to the smallest thing.
The man who passes you on the street and catches your

*eye. Does he know you? Did you go to high school to-
gether, or is he a stranger?*

*Is he a homicidal maniac who hates your guts on sight,
or is he thinking about robbing you?*

*Or is he just some poor guy trying to make a homosex-
ual advance?*

Down the street Charles the anorexic turned and
watched Hobbes disappear into his building. He
sauntered back in that direction.

Or is it nothing, nothing at all?

Hobbes keyed the lock and entered his apartment.
He stopped short. Cryptic conspiratorial voices. Silence. More voices.

He quietly closed the front door and moved warily
down the unlit hallway. That man outside looking at
him in that strange way; now strange voices coming
from his living room. He was fully ready for mon-
strous creatures to come leaping from the darkness.

At the end of the hall Hobbes stepped decisively
into the living room.

Art and Sam had fallen asleep in front of the TV,
which was playing some black-and-white film noir.
Sam was clutching a teddy bear.

Hobbes smiled slightly. He shook his head at his
own hyper-suggestibility.

CHAPTER 24

The D train traveled between Uptown, where Hobbes lived, down into city center, where Castle Street and the nightclub district were located, and terminated one stop farther along at the Lincoln Station Hub. The route looped past the General Motors assembly plant on Van Ness Boulevard, where shift workers poured onto the train, headed for the Hub. At the Hub they would change trains and disperse toward their homes all over the South Side.

The 14th Street subway station was the stop for Castle Street. When the train squealed to a halt there and the doors swooshed open, Charles the anorexic stood wedged between two commuters. He had been squeezed between them since the crowd of workers got on at the GM plant.

One of the two commuters was a fat man with a lunch pail, nicknamed Mouse Face, a transmission assembly specialist.

Mouse Face had gotten his nickname as a kid, from a camp counselor at the Y day camp. Cruel. The counselor was a teenaged bully who liked picking on the smallest, most frightened, weaseliest kid in the group. He got regular laughs from the other kids by treating Mouse Face like a pet rodent. The name stuck like a bad smell. Mouse Face was Mouse Face

at home and on the play yards all the way through
school, even after he'd grown fat and unmouselike.

Still withdrawn, a dud with girls, a wretched student, he found release during his teen years driving
country roads and shooting cats, dogs, road signs
and the occasional calf with a scoped hunting rifle.

He had a reputation at the plant as a short fuse
and a loner. One young guy who tried to befriend
him got a busted cheek for sticking his nose into
Mouse Face's business.

That blowup had been a year before. At the time,
the Human Relations officer offered for the plant to
pay for free counseling for Mouse Face. Surprisingly,
he accepted the offer and, more surprisingly, seemed
to benefit from it. He was apparently working
through his rage, and actually making a few friends
at the plant. He was a success story.

This night he was tired and irritable when he got
on the train. He had been picked on unfairly by a
supervisor, and he was trying not to take it personally. But he was bruised, feeling ornery; like the old
Mouse Face.

Something had happened on the ride down. By the
time Charles the anorexic slid out from between
Mouse Face and the other auto workers and got off,
something had definitely happened.

Charles hit the platform, looked around uncertainly for a second, then walked toward the street
stairs.

Mouse Face watched him through the window as
the D train rolled on, headed for the Hub. He had a
little smile on his face.

CHAPTER 25

Hobbes communed with a single can of beer for a while in his kitchen, letting his flywheel spin down. He got up from the table, threw the beer can in the trash and made his way into the living room.

The black-and-white detective story was still playing. Hobbes snapped it off and gently shook Art.

His brother turned, disoriented. "Johnny?" he said.

"Time to go to sleep, Art," Hobbes said. "Come on, pull down Sammy's covers."

Hobbes picked up the boy from the couch. Art stood up and padded on ahead, wiping sleep from his eyes with his knuckles like a little kid.

As they moved down the hall, the phone rang. Art automatically picked up the hall extension as he passed.

"Hello?" he said. ". . . Hello?"

Nobody answering at the other end. Without any reaction, Art hung up. These calls were such a routine occurrence that Art barely noticed them now. And Hobbes did not have to comment.

They made their way into Art's and Sam's bedroom in the dark, picking their way through Sammy's clothes and sports equipment on the floor.

At Charles's apartment not far from the mini-golf on Castle Street, a key turned in the lock and Charles walked in. Realizing he was famished, he had stopped at the market on the corner and bought food. He put down his two bags of groceries and glanced around. The place was immaculate.

A moment of confusion. He walked through the place, looking. He dropped his jacket on the floor, his hat on the couch.

Art pulled down Sammy's covers. Hobbes laid the boy on the bed.

The phone started ringing again.

Art pulled the covers up and smoothed them over the boy's sleeping form. He looked at the boy for a moment.

Hobbes watched from the doorway.

Art looked up at him and said quietly, "Johnny? . . . You ever get scared?"

"Sometimes," Hobbes said. Art's brain was damaged, he wasn't stupid. Hobbes knew Art would know instantly if Hobbes wasn't telling him the truth. So he always did, he never tried to sugarcoat; instead he tried to reassure by his manner.

Art nodded. The phone kept ringing. The room was very dark.

"Me, too," Art said.

The phone stopped. Silence filled the empty space.

Charles stood at the stove, making himself a grilled cheese sandwich. The lonely guy special. The ingredients were spread around the counter in his normal messy way.

He glanced at the phone as if remembering something. He picked it up, dialed as he cooked.

"Mrs. Moohr?" he said into the phone. "This is Charles. Apparently . . . I must've gotten drunk or something, 'cause the last few days . . . I don't know. Am I working tonight?"

"You quit, Charles," he heard Mrs. Moohr's voice say.

"I quit?"

"You insulted Harry, and he hired someone else," she said.

Charles stared uncomprehendingly at the cupboard in front of him. "Oh," was all he could manage.

The doorbell rang.

Charles headed for the door, cordless phone at his ear. "Look," he said. "I'm really sorry, I . . . Could you apologize please to your husband for whatever I . . ."

Mrs. Moohr sounded a little taken aback. "I will, Charles," she said. "Thank you, we . . . we always liked you." Abruptly, she hung up.

Charles heard a dial tone. He pressed OFF on the phone and unlocked his door.

A violent force burst in. A man, but a man possessed by the most primitive homicidal fury, wielding a weapon, lunging with it. The weapon, wrapped in his fist, was a large hypodermic needle.

The attacker plunged the needle in, again and again, like a knife, fluid flying out the tip. Sprays of blood. Savage, uncontrollable torrent of blows, different parts of the body, head, heart, pounding, smashing . . .

Charles fought back, waving his arms ineffectually, slapping at the intruder. Useless. The attack was relentless, without quarter.

Charles staggered back, fell.

Like a wild beast the attacker leapt in for the kill. Just before he went, Charles half recognized his

assailant, felt he knew him. From somewhere . . .
From somewhere so recently? . . .

Hobbes was sitting in front of his TV-VCR, studying the videotape made at the prison. The section
with Reese muttering incoherently. Hobbes jotted
something down in a small notebook.

The phone rang.

Hobbes picked it up, listened and heard nothing.
He held the receiver away from him. He then turned
it toward the TV so the person listening could hear
Reese's voice. A dark joke. One he felt instinctively
was the right one. He couldn't say why, not logically.

The attacker—Mouse Face—walked around Charles's
apartment, eating the man's grilled cheese sandwich,
holding a cordless phone to his ear. Smiling. Saying
nothing.

As he moved back and forth in the small living
room, he passed the open door to the bathroom and
looked in at his work. In the bathtub Charles's nude
body lay stiffening, a shocked look frozen on his face.

Mouse Face returned to the kitchen and hung up
the phone. He took milk from the fridge and a box
of corn flakes from the cabinet.

He carried the breakfast things to the table and set
them down.

Looked at them.

Adjusted the angles.

CHAPTER 26

In the precinct squad room Hobbes was up for Loony of the Day. He sat hunched at his desk with files open and piled around him. He was boning up on a case. Not a current case. Not an open case. A dead case by the name of Reese.

His desk was piled with stuff about the late psychopath. Photos, newspaper clippings, investigative reports, psychiatric assessments, coroner's reports and more. Hobbes was leafing through it, a slow, contemplative process. He sensed something was there, he could smell it. He was going to follow his instinct despite a good bit of ribbing from the likes of Lou and Lawrence.

Jonesy drifted over. "I played Reese's tape on the phone to a linguist guy," he said. "He's coming down."

"Prelim?" Hobbes said.

"Says it sounds Middle Eastern," Jonesy said.

"Any more on Muskavich?"

"Only his pizza," Jonesy said.

Lou was passing by. "Hitting your area of expertise, huh, Jonesy?" he said with a smirk.

Jonesy turned on Lou with mock earnestness. "Look, man," he said. "Pizza is the staff of life. Without pizza and other fine Italian foods, there is no happiness, okay?" Delivered with the absolute conviction of a Jihad true believer.

He turned back to Hobbes. "There was one slice left," he said. "Deep dish: garlic, Linguisa and pineapple. An unusual combo. But Sal's on 23rd on the South Side has it—a number 17. I just happen to know. I depo-ed a witness on that block last year."

"You oughta put a pizza map of the city in the department computer, Jonesy," Hobbes said. "No foolin'."

"Plus," Jonesy said, "there was nothin' in Muskavich's stomach, so it was definitely the killer's eats."

"You're saying the killer might live around there?"

"It's a shot," Jonesy said.

"Hell of a clue, Jonesy," Lou said. "Better write this up for the journal."

Jonesy stared at him blankly. "I will, Lou," he said finally. "And if I do, I will laud you copiously."

Hobbes had returned to his Reese case files. He was deep into the man's background folder: childhood photos, old letters, school reports, a sports clipping from a high school newspaper.

"Hey," Jonesy said.

Hobbes looked up.

Jonesy nodded toward the door. A tall, bespectacled angular man was just coming in.

The linguist is here," Jonesy said, getting up to meet the man.

"Be right there," Hobbes said.

Jonesy nodded, and Hobbes went back to his research. A series of photos, the eyes of a killer. Then Hobbes's eyes narrowed. He remembered seeing something that bothered him. He dug back and found the old sports clipping from a high school newspaper, a photo of Reese in a batter's stance.

Hobbes stared at it: Reese in a batter's crouch at the left side of the plate, glaring toward the pitcher's mound, expectant. Something about the picture didn't make sense.

He stared at it thoughtfully a moment longer, put it in the middle of his desk and headed off down the hall.

In the video room Jonesy and Richard Louders, a linguist, were watching the documentary tape of Reese as Hobbes entered.

"Any luck?" Hobbes said.

Jonesy waved his hand. "John Hobbes, Professor Richard Louders."

"Formidable!" Louders muttered at the TV screen at the same moment. It was immediately apparent to Hobbes what kind of duck the bespectacled Louders was: a chromedome who got maximum mileage out of being a Frenchman among Americans. To him it was a license to behave with flair and eccentricity. "This is completely exhilarating," Louders enthused. "Who is this man, some kind of convict?"

"The professor says it's a language all right," Jonesy said, "but he's never heard it spoken before."

"Meaning?" Hobbes said.

Jonesy shrugged. "It's some kinda antique."

Louders spoke with gestures. "I believe this is a biblical tongue," he said, "Syrian Aramaic. Only a few nomadic tribes still use it." What a delight. *"Un rêve. Quel joie!"*

"So you don't know what he's saying?" Hobbes said. "Let's get to the facts."

Louders gave a grand Gallic shrug. "Haven't the faintest *idée*." He continued to watch Reese's behavior closely. "The gestures aren't too *plaisant*, are they?" He looked up at Hobbes hopefully. "If you could spare me a copy," he said, "I'd be more than happy to work it."

Hobbes saw no *probleme*.

Jonesy nodded. "Hey. Appreciate that, huh?" he said, standing. He walked Louders to the door. "If you can hang about fifteen minutes, we'll make you a dupe."

" 'ang? . . ." Louders murmured. "Ah, hang! *Bien sûr!*" He went out to the waiting room to do just that.

Hobbes rewound the tape back to Reese and the priest. He turned off the sound, ran it forward and watched.

Jonesy returned. "*Aramaic?*" he said.

Hobbes shook his head in wonder. "I know," he said. He was playing over and over a short section in which Reese beckoned for the priest to come in and get killed.

The documentary camera was cutting back and forth from Reese's leering face to the priest's face, revealing his faltering resolve. The priest then turned and spoke quietly to the guard, who unlocked the outer door for him. The priest left. With the sound off, Reese's mouth can be seen yelling, "Coward! How can you serve God if you ain't got any balls?!" Reese pivoted and spoke to the camera—to Hobbes: "Johnny boy, you watching?" He waved.

Jonesy didn't get it at all. "Edgar Reese drove a bus," he said. "He was smart, but self-educated, so a little Dutch? Maybe. But some ancient tongue only a few tribesmen speak?"

"I found something else," Hobbes said. "In Reese's file was a clipping from his high school baseball team. He batted right, threw right."

They watched the tape. Reese was gesturing and waving with his left hand.

"So," Jonesy said. "He bats right and waves left."

Hobbes backed up the tape, turned up the sound at the point where Reese was saying, "Johnny boy, you watching?" He waved at the camera. "I hope you're paying close attention . . . every gesture, every word . . ."

Jonesy leaned down and stopped the tape, ejected it. "We gotta get this duped," he said.

They both walked toward the door.

"What're you saying, Hobbes?" Jonesy asked, meaning the left-right–handedness.

They were headed back to their desks. Louders was visible through the partition, waiting out in the anteroom.

"I mean, Reese did some of the sickest shit on record," Jonesy said. "He's speaking a language two thousand years old. And you're worried 'cause he's ambidextrous?"

Hobbes's phone rang.

"I'm worried about everything," he said, picking up the phone. "John Hobbes," he said into the mouthpiece.

"Hey, pal," a voice said. "Need another clue?" It was Mouse Face.

Hobbes was silent. He did not recognize the voice. This was not the same caller who had said, "It's a clue, Magoo."

"1339 South Grove, apartment 9," Mouse Face said.

Then a dial tone.

Hobbes looked at Jonesy, who had returned to his desk opposite.

"That pizza place," Hobbes said, "with the number 17?"

Jonesy lit up. "You want a pie?" he said, pleased. He was hungry. Jonesy was always hungry, especially for pie.

"Is it close to Grove Street?" Hobbes said.

Oh. Just more business. Jonesy was crestfallen.

CHAPTER 27

Charles's apartment at dusk was a dismal place at the best of times. Cramped and ill-lit. Never very clean, always in desperate need of a paint job.

Now it was a horrifying mess, the wreckage of a struggle. Furniture overturned. Broken glass, liquids spilled, plant dirt spread across the floor. A bookshelf knocked half over. Food on the kitchen floor.

One of the other things Hobbes noticed as he and Jonesy passed the kitchen was a half-eaten grilled cheese sandwich on the counter. Lonely guy special.

They walked into the bathroom. A gaunt male body lay face up in the bathtub. Nude.

Toothbrush and toothpaste were lined up tidily on the sink. Recently used. Hobbes bent down. A faint odor of toothpaste came from the sink.

Charles's clothes were piled haphazardly in the middle of the floor.

A coroner's technician turned the skinny body so he could look at the back. He turned it face up again. On the dead man's face, arms and chest: puncture marks. And written in black magic marker on the scrawny chest, the number 2.

Charles the anorexic. His eyes were wide open, a look of terror etched in them.

Hobbes looked at Charles and reacted; looked close

at his face. He glanced at Jonesy, then back at Charles.

Hobbes's half dollar appeared in his right hand and was going a mile a minute. The worry-bead object that came to his hand almost automatically when anxiety welled up. Now a nameless dread was orbiting in his skull.

Hobbes moved with Jonesy out of the bathroom, through the trashed living room, back to the seedy kitchen. Rust-stained sink, cracked formica countertops. The leavings of the grilled cheese sandwich.

And a kitchen table with just four things on it: a box of cornflakes, a container of milk, a sugar bowl and a half-eaten bowl of cereal.

A shrieking buzzer went off in the heads of both Hobbes and Jonesy.

What set it off was the way the four objects were placed. Carefully aligned in the same distinctive configuration as at Muskavich's.

"They're in the same place," Jonesy said quietly. "Exact."

"Yeah," Hobbes said.

"Like he's laughin' at us," Jonesy said somberly.

Hobbes turned toward the wall opposite the table where, at the murdered Russian's flat, they had found a magic marker scrawl—the riddle about the space between Lyons and Spakowsky. This time there was a mirror there. Hobbes was relieved. Enough was enough.

He started scoping out the rest of the place. But it gnawed at him. What if—?

Just in case, highly unlikely, but—

Casually, he went back to the wall opposite the kitchen table and moved the mirror aside. Jonesy watched him.

Jesus. There was writing underneath it.

Dreading it, Hobbes pushed the mirror farther. Writing all right, a message, but a different message. This one said:

??? = look in mirror

Hobbes stared at it. The scrawl in Muskavich's apartment flashed back in his mind:

Lyons
???
Spakowsky

Hobbes was the first to speak. "What's he saying? The guy in the middle, Robert Milano's, got something to do with me?"

Jonesy shrugged, wide-eyed. Even that inference was beyond him.

Hobbes looked around the place, shaking his head in bewilderment. "You know what's scary?" he said.

Jonesy looked a little in shock. "Huh," he said. What *isn't* scary in all of this? he was thinking.

"Last night, going home," Hobbes said, "a guy walking the other way looked me in the eye. One of those looks like he knows you, you know?"

Jonesy nodded: Yeah, so?

Hobbes didn't want to say it. He wanted to bury it. "It was the guy in the bathtub," he said. "The stiff."

"You're shitting me," Jonesy said.

"Uh-uh."

"Hey, man," Jonesy said. "I'm not smart enough to figure out what's going down here."

"Makes two of us," Hobbes said. None of this was adding up to anything in the range of Hobbes's experience. He could not construct a theory to fit all the weirdo facts these murders were throwing up.

A forensics guy, Bill Clark, came up to Hobbes and held out the large hypodermic syringe that Mouse Face had wielded like a dagger. It still had some liquid left in it. Clark, who was wearing double-thickness latex evidence gloves, had a Ziploc evidence bag ready.

"Big surprise," Hobbes said, slipping on latex gloves and taking the syringe gingerly.

"From under the couch," Clark said.

Hobbes carefully unscrewed the top of the needle. He moved his nose closer. Didn't smell anything. Closer. When his nose got right up to the top, he reacted slightly.

"Same poison?" Jonesy said. "Stuff'd kill an elephant less than a minute."

Hobbes handed the syringe back to Clark. "Get this to the lab."

Clark zip-locked it in and headed off.

"What else?" Hobbes said to Jonesy, looking around.

"The number on his chest?" Jonesy said. " 'Eighteen' was Thursday, now he's at 'two'?"

Hobbes shrugged. Again, things they were seeing with their eyes that didn't fit with any reality he knew.

The coroner's men went by, carrying Charles's body wrapped in a body bag.

Lou came in from questioning the landlord and neighbors.

"Who is this guy anyway?" Hobbes said, watching the dead man go off on his last ride. Seemed like he'd been doing nothing but watching dead men recently.

"Everything's under Charles Olom," Lou said,

"but it looks like some kinda alias. We're running his prints."

Hobbes nodded. Turned. He found his own image staring back from the mirror. The look on his face would have scared a witch doctor.

CHAPTER 28

Hobbes was at his desk in the precinct, cogitating. Trying out different theories why an accomplice or accomplices of Reese would be pulling this stuff. What did they have to gain? Taunting Hobbes just wasn't motive enough, it couldn't be. Murder takes too much effort.

No, something else was going on, he was sure of it.

And he was being drawn along by a carrot dangling from a string. He knew that what he had to do was jump ahead of the dangling bait and figure out the game before somebody else died.

Reese had filled his mind, and the filmmakers' videotape, with clues. To what? Why was he having such a hard time breaking the code? He was famous for being able to see the pattern in the welter of detail. Where was it this time? What sick scheme was he being made to play a part in?

Or had he just gone around the bend on this whole thing; giving Reese far too much credit for reaching his long arm out of his potter's field grave? He stared off into space.

I couldn't let it rest. Are you kidding? There is a basic human need to know. You can count on it. An unquenchable thirst.

Something's lurking just outside your vision, just out-

side your knowledge—you sense it's there, and you must look.

Look, find, and see it, whatever it may be. Wherever it may lead.

Jonesy was like the yellow line down the side of the road for Hobbes. When he got too wound up and started veering toward a ditch, Jonesy was there to give him a jab and remind him he was only a cop, not a priest; it was only a job, not the Crusades.

Jonesy had been born tough and raised hard by two mill workers. His father yanked him out of school for a year at thirteen when his mother got sick. Somebody had to take care of his five-year-old brother and two-year-old sister.

He grew big and sinewy and became a football standout at powerhouse McKinley High on the South Side. Offensive center and rangy defensive nose tackle both. Nobody came through his part of the line; he was a wall. McKinley was Triple A Division champion all four of Jonesy's years. He was captain his last two years.

He got some college feelers his junior and senior years, but he wasn't interested in doing anything but being a cop. It wasn't a family thing. It was a chance bit of reading he did on the team bus going to an away game. The coach lent him his copy of Truman Capote's *In Cold Blood.*

Jonesy was so gripped by the story and by the incredible dedication of the Kansas detectives who tracked down and brought the murderers to justice, he came away with a passion to do what those guys did for a living.

To hell with football and reading *Beowulf* and *The Faerie Queene* in college.

H went to work in a box factory, driving forklift and saving his money. After several years he enrolled at the John Jay College of Criminal Justice in New York. Armed with a criminology degree, he beat it back to his home city and went straight into the police academy.

Jonesy reveled in copdom. Even being a beat patrolman in a radio car. He was known as one of those cops who never "carried" jobs—delayed reporting he was done on one so he could sift through incoming assignments and take his pick of the cushy ones.

Unlike a lot of cops, he never avoided domestic dispute calls. He had a gift for talking to any and all kinds of people in high states of anger or agitation. The legend was he could talk down Leona Helmsley if the situation called for it.

"Call me a radio whore," Jonesy used to say about his appetite for jobs. "If Central's got it for sale, I'll buy."

"Fixers," though—fixed posts guarding prisoners in court or at a hospital—were not for Jonesy. His whole big body would start to vibrate with bottled-up energy.

Jonesy and Hobbes made detective the same year, and they'd been working the same "cold critters" ever since. Jonesy was the ideal partner, so far as Hobbes was concerned. The big guy was absolutely fearless. He was never known to take a step back, and was always ready to take two more forward.

Actually, Jonesy was afraid of one thing.

When Lieutenant Stanton leaned out and called from his office, Jonesy hopped to and went in with flags flying and all pistons firing. He was afraid of any boss who could take away his job being a police detective.

* * *

Stanton's door at the far end of the squad room was open. Jonesy was inside, talking to the man.

"Well," Jonesy said, "to quote Yogi Berra: It's like déjà vu all over again."

"You mean Reese?" Stanton said.

"Yeah," Jonesy said.

"And whoever's doing it has a thing for Hobbes?" the lieutenant said.

Jonesy shrugged. "Seems like."

Stanton looked out the door toward Hobbes's desk in the middle of the room. "How is he?" he asked.

"Hobbes?" Jonesy said. "How is he ever? He's fine."

"Well, if it starts to work at him," Stanton said, "lemme know, okay?"

"Yeah," Jonesy said, adding with a grin, "and if it starts to work at me, I'll tell you that, too, huh?"

Jonesy ambled out and back toward his desk. By the time he got there, Hobbes was gone.

But not far.

In the precinct public area the duty sergeant's desk was behind a low wooden railing that kept the citizens over there and the cops over here.

Hobbes came out from the squad room, went to the peg board behind the desk and removed a key on a wooden stick from a hook. He headed for the basement stairway.

He emerged into the basement area with lockers and showers at one end. A few cops were in there on shift change, talking and joking.

Hobbes made his way toward the other end of the basement, the evidence and general storage areas. It was there he and Lou had found the Cop of the Year plaque, behind the thick old iron-link fencing.

Hobbes unlocked the back area and walked in, surveying the chaotic collection of file cabinets, cardboard storage boxes, evidence racks.

He examined the labels on the file cabinets: Homicide 1983. Homicide 1982 . . .

He found the year he needed, pulled the box down and sat on the floor near the fencing where the light was best. He started methodically going through the contents of a cardboard storage box.

He stopped on a printed page, a report, and read from it. ". . . *As the three detectives approached Milano's cabin, they heard a gunshot . . .*" Hobbes read on, scanning the next few pages of the report.

He found a photograph: a body sprawled out, face first, on a kitchen floor.

He turned the following page and saw a map. He was examining it when he sensed something. He looked up—

Lou, standing on the other side of the fence, was in his gym clothes; he had been working out.

"I heard a noise," he said. Looking at the map in Hobbes's hands, he said, "Whattaya doin', historical research?"

Hobbes nodded and turned over the map so Lou couldn't see it.

Lou took a long curious gander at the cardboard box Hobbes was digging through. Finally: "See you tomorrow, huh?" he said. He gave Hobbes a look and strolled back down the hall.

What was that all about? Hobbes thought. Lou was an insecure guy. It made him intrusive, nosy, always worried that other cops were getting better assignments, better info, better equipment than he. He wanted to know what everybody was doing. He was a pain in the ass.

Was that all he was doing, or was there more to it? Was his interest in Hobbes's doings just his usual paranoid nosiness, or something else?

Hobbes cautioned himself to lighten up a little here. He'd known Lou for six months. He was just a blustery cop.

You do everything. That's all you can do, all anyone can ask of you—including yourself.

Hobbes went back to studying the map.

Robert Milano. A body on a kitchen floor. A map to a cabin. Some kind of clue or link—but what the hell is it?

An idea was forming in Hobbes's head. It would probably be a dead end, but at least it was something he could *do*. Some action he could take instead of just stewing about this bizarre and brutal series of crimes, and waiting for the next chess move by the maniac who was trying to torment him.

He folded the map and put it in his pocket.

CHAPTER 29

Playground basketball. It could be played at the highest levels, and also at the Hobbes family level, which was close to headlong chaos.

The morning's game was three-on-three, one adult to a side. Definitely on the chaos level. A successful game was one in which everybody walked away in one piece.

Art was "broadcasting" the action from the sideline, Hobbes heading up the team of Sam and his buddy Toby. Against a neighborhood dad and two other kids. That dad, Ron, a little overweight and sweating, was happy to be as laid back about the contest as Hobbes and give the kids the starring roles.

Art's rap befit the game. Scattershot and fractured. He tried to report every single thing that happened, regardless of importance. He was particularly focused on dribbling.

"Johnny goes right, comes back left," Art called out, "passes to Sam, Sam dribbles. Keeps dribbling. Around Ernie. Sam dribbling still. The score is tied, folks—"

"No, it's not!" Toby yelled, jumping up and down at the right of the key with arms high signaling for a pass.

"The score is not tied," Art barked. "Sammy is

dribbling around the top of the key, looking for an open man . . ."

"It's 19-17!" Sam called out.

"The score is 19-17?" Art said. "Who's ahead?"

"We are!" Sam yelled.

"Okay," Art called. "Okay. *We* are ahead. Who has the ball? Toby! Toby is dribbling. Toby dribbles into the lane, he's going to shoot—wait a minute—"

Art: disoriented. Because very quickly Toby had slipped a pass to Hobbes underneath, who passed to Sam out by the foul line who shot and scored. All partially obscured from Art's view. Too fast.

"What happened," Art said, "did we—?"

Sam, Toby and Hobbes were jumping, cheering.

Art shouted: "We won! We won the game! The Hobbes and Toby team come up winners! A hard-fought game on both sides, sports fans. Excellent winning shot by . . . who got that shot? . . ."

"That was great, guys," Hobbes called out to the other team. "Thanks a lot."

"Please, Mr. Hobbes, one more?" Toby said.

"Come on, Unc—" Sam said pleadingly.

"I can't, Sammy," Hobbes said. "I got a long drive. Get your dad in here."

Sam glanced sideways at Art. "But he's a spaz," he said softly.

Hobbes gave him a look there was no mistaking.

"I'm sorry, I know," Sammy said. "I . . ."

Hobbes noticed a bulky form approaching. Jonesy, with his work face on. "Cherish what you got, kid," Hobbes said to Sammy.

Sam called to Toby: "Hey—it's his partner."

Toby, watching Hobbes walk toward Jonesy, made a little swagger move. "Eww," he said, "the man."

Hobbes baited his out-of-shape ex-athlete partner

gently. "You want some of this?" he said. "Hey, I'm leaving."

"I didn't bring my shoes," Jonesy said with mock regret. Then: "Tiffany didn't get you?"

"I left my beeper," Hobbes said. "What gives?"

"You know how weird this case is?" the fat man said.

Hobbes couldn't believe it: There was more to add on the weirdness level? "Say it," he said.

"We got an ID on 'Charles Olom'," Jonesy said. "Real name Mickey Noons, born in Canada, illegal alien, small-time shithead."

"That's not bad," Hobbes said.

Jonesy shook his head. "That's not it," he said. "Noons is the guy who killed the Roosky. It's his prints all over Muskavich's apartment."

Ka-ching. Something immediately made an odd sense about that in Hobbes's mind.

"Noons poisons Muskavich," Jonesy said, "dumps him in the tub and sets out the cornflakes. Three days later somebody does the exact same thing to Noons. Exact."

Hobbes nodded. "Yeah," he said. "Exact. 'Cause Noons and Muskavich were actually killed by the same person."

"Some third person?" Jonesy was swimming upstream here. "Some kinda ringmaster?"

"I think so," Hobbes said.

"Who," Jonesy said. *"Who?"*

"I don't know," Hobbes said. He couldn't quite get his mind around that part yet. Not even close. "But I got a bad feeling."

"Me, too," Jonesy said dourly. "Like somebody's playin' with my dick and it ain't me."

CHAPTER 30

Hobbes drove across the suspension bridge leaving the city. Not a lot of traffic going north that time of morning.

He drove an hour and a quarter before the road started to rise and wind its way up into the rolling mountains. The two-lane blacktop curved around the shoulders of scrub-covered hills and cut through rock passes as it climbed into the back country. Soon he was in the old-growth forest, among the wind-bent pines and deciduous giants in the full glory of their late fall foliage.

The landscape was gorgeous: the dark evergreens, the elms and maples red, orange and gold against patches of early snow. But it was also desolate. No settlements, few isolated houses; then no more houses. Just woods, silence and more woods.

As the road passed through a particularly narrow rocky gorge, pines towered close above and blotted out the light, and Hobbes had the sudden sensation he was in spooky alien territory.

He drove over a bridge crossing a tumbling river. A solid steel-and-concrete span built not too many years before. Reassuring.

But then the road narrowed again, the shoulder

disappeared, the forest squeezing in on the highway, yielding right-of-way reluctantly.

By and by the paved road petered out entirely. Hobbes checked his regular route map and drove on. Travel was now over a packed dirt road that was graded for blacktop but never finished.

Half an hour later the road forked. Unpaved, rutted county roads tracked off in both directions. No signposts, no aids to the wayfarer.

Hobbes consulted the hand-drawn map he had taken from the basement files. He smoothed it out and studied it for long minutes before choosing the left fork and proceeding uncertainly.

The ever-dwindling county dirt road was now little more than a fire road through the wilderness. Hobbes in his old Plymouth jounced on for miles, checking the crude map every few minutes. In a wooded valley he passed a scarred wooden signpost, its sign long since shot to pieces by drive-by marksmen.

A few hundred yards farther down the road, Hobbes braked to a halt. He put the car into reverse and backed up to the signpost. Almost hidden in the undergrowth was the beginning of a driveway.

He turned in and drove down a long dirt and gravel drive that curved among white pines and junipers and tall sugar maples. His car bumped over patches of wild grass and burdock weeds, scraped through encroaching lilac and elderberry thickets.

The Plymouth came out in a clearing facing the pinewood log cabin that had belonged to Robert Milano.

Hobbes rolled the car slowly toward the dwelling, taking in the bucolic scene. The Queen Anne's lace along the sides of the house, the path down to the lake, the breeze-rippled water stretching across toward a woodsy autumnal shore.

It was as quiet as a church sacristy. It felt to Hobbes just as holy, a place that ought to be safe from all things profane and sinister.

He knew better.

He parked the Plymouth and stepped out, his eyes drawn to the lake water glittering away toward the far shore, his ears drawn to the soothing liquid sounds of small waves lapping on rocks. He was momentarily mesmerized, lulled.

So much so, he didn't see an animal scurry under the cabin steps. Was it a cat? Hobbes never laid eyes on it.

He turned toward the high-peaked, two-story frame structure. He imagined it in its pristine state— handsome, sturdy, pleasingly consonant with its sylvan surroundings.

Not at all pristine now. Depressingly broken-down. Screens ripped out. Weeds pushing through cracks in the foundation.

The wind kicked up a notch, stirring the lake, piling leaves against the stone foundation of the cabin, creating a disquieting effect in Hobbes.

He walked around the house to a small dock. Wind-ruffled water slapped against the rotting pilings. The boards creaked and gave as he stepped on the dock.

He turned and surveyed the cabin. Windows were broken out on the lake side, shot out by drunken hunters, stoned out by marauding kids.

He didn't like the feeling of the place. Something was telling him, don't turn over this rock. Get in your car and drive back to the dirty, noisy, familiar city.

I think people find the hardest thing of all is to just keep going. Know what I mean?

You don't know what's there, but you sense something—just beyond your vision, just outside your reach.

Hobbes gave himself a kick: Cut the crap. He started toward the cabin.

CHAPTER 31

Though the sun shone white and glaring outside, the interior of Milano's house was dark, the windows covered with decades of grime. Hobbes flicked a switch, but the electricity was off.

He pulled a flashlight from his leather jacket and shined it around. The rooms felt creepy, smelled musty. Were there rats living there? Snakes? Monsters?

Old summerhouse wooden and wicker furniture spoke of a happier time.

A mirror on the wall was so sullied it cast a barely recognizable reflection when Hobbes stood before it.

Hobbes looked around the kitchen. It was barren, empty of every utensil, cleaned out—no signs left behind of its having been enjoyed by a family for years of seasonal outings.

Hobbes noticed light-colored marks on the floor, a pattern of some sort. He scuffed away years of accumulated dirt and leaves. Gradually, to creepy effect, the taped outline of a sprawled body became visible. Police tape. Homicide tape. This is where Milano died.

Hobbes climbed the narrow, steep interior stairs. A tiny wood-railinged balcony looked down on the first floor.

He checked out the three upstairs rooms.

Diminutive bed frames in the two smaller rooms—children's bedrooms. Small empty bureaus next to both beds. A protruding "closet" that had a piece of cloth hanging at the front as a door of sorts.

Hobbes went into the larger bedroom. It had the same kind of closets. The cloth on one of them was pulled aside so Hobbes could see inside. A few clothes hung there: men's clothes, a work shirt, overalls, a dingy bathrobe.

Hobbes walked across the dimly illuminated space. Nothing on the walls, not so much as a drugstore calendar. As he moved toward the window, the cloth covering the other closet moved slightly. Something or someone was behind it.

Hobbes drew his gun from the holster behind his hip.

He moved toward the closet.

Again, very slightly, the cloth moved.

Hobbes yanked the cloth aside—

No one there. No clothes even. Just an open window in the room. The floor covered with many autumns' worth of sugar maple leaves, now brown and dessicated.

On the desk in the living room Hobbes found some old photos. He shined his flashlight on one of them. A grandmother with a bunch of grown children and young grandchildren.

He picked up another photo. A family: Milano, his wife and a three-month-old child. A joyous—now ironically joyous—image.

He studied the faces. The wife was the spitting image of Gretta. Gretta's mother, of course. And the three-month-old Gretta. Same big serious eyes.

He replaced the photographs and looked aimlessly

around the living room. The truth was, he had no idea what he was looking for up here.

It was Reese's doing, of course. Reese had pointed him in Milano's direction, and Milano's story led straight to this place and ended here.

For Hobbes, one logical assumption was that Milano's secrets—whatever led him to take his own life—could well be here where he did the deed.

Another logical assumption was that Reese wanted Hobbes to find out the story on Milano. Why? Because Reese's posthumous murders were somehow linked to Milano, now thirty years dead? How? And where did Hobbes fit in all this?

Though Hobbes felt he was probably walking into a trap of some kind—if only one of Reese's mind-fucks—he didn't feel he had any choice. How else to get to the bottom of the killings and stop any more from being done?

Hobbes wandered into the hallway. He glanced at the refrigerator, which was in the hall just outside the kitchen. Boxes were piled beside it. Behind the boxes Hobbes now noticed a doorway.

He cleared away the boxes and opened the door. Cellar stairs. He picked his way down the stairs in the gloaming, shining his flashlight ahead of him.

Milano had transformed the basement into a study of sorts.

A desk, papers, files, a bulletin board. On the wall was a diagram: a list of names, including the Ivy League Killer, Milano's biggest case, with arrows pointing from one name to another. Hobbes stared at it, realizing: Milano worked down here.

Hobbes examined the wall diagram; looked through some old duplicate police case files; riffled

through a folder of case notes, of personal finances.
He found nothing on the desk of any interest.

A shelf of law books and true-crime books. He
thumbed through them. Nothing there.

It was a dead end after all. Hobbes looked around
in frustration. He had found nothing in the house
that hinted at why Milano had killed himself; and
nothing even remotely related to Reese.

Hobbes chewed on himself for letting his imagination get the better of him.

He passed the flashlight once more around the
basement, swept it across the rafter beams above
his head.

Something caught his eye.

Probably nothing, but he walked closer, shining
the light upward. Wedged above one of the two-by-
six floor supports, entangled in old vines intruding
through the cracked cement sidewall, were a bunch
of old books—six or seven, leather-bound, some of
them; dusty, almost invisible from below.

Hobbes got up on a chair, pushed aside the thick
vines and took a book down. He rested it on the
desk and glanced through it.

He shined his light up among the vines, took the
other books down, and laid them out carefully on
the desk.

They were hardcover books, some very old, archi-
val tomes. And, in subject matter, *not* the kinds of
books Hobbes expected to find in the study of the
straightedge, all-business, street cop Milano was supposed to have been.

There were religious art texts, a Bible, a large-
format art book with slip of paper sticking out of it.
Hobbes opened the book at the paper and saw the

famous image from the Sistine Chapel: God reaching out with his forefinger to touch Adam, to give life.

He examined the covers of the other books: volumes on the beliefs and mystical lore and practices of ancient civilizations.

He picked up one of these, and as he began to leaf through it, he heard something inhuman, a remote, unidentifiable sound, almost subliminal.

He looked up, uneasy.

What Hobbes heard might have been a deep rumble from an animal throat, from somewhere within the walls or beyond them. But not likely. Probably it was just the wind stressing the weathered timbers of the old cabin, causing the lumber to settle. Old buildings grumbled and moved; it was a perfectly natural process.

He went back to the book, flipping through pages, past images of tribal gods, shamans, priest figures with their amulets and other primitive gear for tribute and appeasement.

He turned another page, and as the new image registered—a hideous demon with a face on its ass— a loud crack reverberated in the small room, then a screech and a roar as the entire section of ceiling in front of him dropped down a foot.

Hobbes lurched backward, startled to the bone. Dust and debris showered down on the space in front of him, pelting everything underneath the dropped ceiling. More groaning in the beams. Hobbes looked for escape, sure he was about to be buried alive.

CHAPTER 32

He was barely touched.

He checked himself: no harm. Cautiously, he shined his flashlight around the rest of the ceiling, looking for cracks, movement in the beams, ready to make a dash for the stairs. Nothing.

It all seemed secure.

He listened, waiting for more telltale noises, then went back to the book. He flipped past the picture of the demon, past images of other evil spirits and depictions of rituals for vanquishing or tricking them.

A loose photograph slipped out of the book. An eight-by-ten sheet of photographic paper. Hobbes examined it, turning it all around. It was a black-and-white photograph, to be sure, but not an easily identifiable image—hard to "read." The exposure was entirely black except for a white oval in the center and, standing partly in front of it, what looked like the edge of an old wooden snow sled slanting in one corner.

Hobbes stared at it, turned it over. On the back, written in faded ink, one word: "Look."

He flipped it over again. At the top edge of the black exposure was a thin white strip. He looked closely. It could be a strip of wall molding.

He looked around pensively. His eyes fell on the far wall. Plain, unadorned, painted dark brown. And where the wall met the ceiling: white molding. Very like the photograph. Fallen on its side on the floor near the wall was a Flexible Flyer snow sled.

Hobbes held up the photo, compared it to the wall. Yes, but one difference was obvious. The wall in front of him had no white oval in the center.

He moved up and ran his hand over the painted surface of the wall, scrutinized it from a side angle.

He stepped back and stared at the wall, at the photograph, turning the photo over: "Look."

A sudden flush swept over him. He felt manipulated and foolish and furious. Here he was dancing like a puppet on a string, following a choreography laid down for him by *Reese*!

Reese before he died.

Was it possible? Could Reese really have pointed him to the Milano case and laid down a trail of beans for him to follow right to these books, this photograph, in this horror-laden place? To what depraved end?

Then he had a second thought.

He looked up at the rafters where the books had been put away. Put where they'd be hard to find, where they'd be found only by someone who had an investment in looking into the Milano affair.

A realization gripped him, a near certainty.

What if he had this backward? What if it wasn't Reese who had thought of everything, but Milano? What if the books and this photograph were a message from Milano—maybe something about the psycho murderer Milano had sent to the gas chamber, the Ivy League Killer? Maybe it was Milano who was waving the hidden material like a warning flag, thirty years later, for only the right person to see.

For Hobbes to see.

He scanned around the basement and saw what he was hoping for: a storage area in one dark corner. Some makeshift shelves were filled with tools, crusted paint cans, old brushes, scrapers, steel wool. And an unopened can of turpentine.

Hobbes picked out a chisel and walked back to the dark brown wall. He chipped away with the tool at the paint in the center of the wall, working to remove the thick outer layer.

When he had chipped off an area a couple of feet square, he grabbed the can of turpentine. He soaked an old rag and swabbed at the dirty brown wall. The remainder of the covering paint began to dissolve away.

Gradually, he was exposing the painted-over shape underneath—a white oval.

But the oval was not entirely white. There were hieroglyphiclike scratches underneath the white paint. As though something was written there.

Hobbes applied more turpentine, rubbed harder, harder. His efforts began to reveal small crooked letters scratched into the wall.

He stepped back and stared at them. Blinked, stared some more.

A Z A Z E L

His mind went blank as he gazed uncomprehendingly at the lettering.

What did it mean? It was obviously Milano's secret message. But whom was he hiding it from? And whom did he intend to find it?

It meant absolutely nothing to Hobbes.

In the cabin above the lakeside screen door banged. Hobbes jumped. The wind, of course, he thought. He listened carefully. Creaking timbers, otherwise silence. He thought he heard small animal paws scamper across the roof. A chill went through him.

He copied the lettering from the wall into his notebook, his mind whirling with questions with no answers. He gathered up Milano's library of strange books. He lugged the musty armload up the stairs and straight out the front door.

Darkness was falling. He jammed the outer door closed and headed for his car. Out of there. The sooner the better.

His tires spun on the gravel, and he nosed his car out the long, overgrown serpentine driveway.

He left with greater uneasiness clutching at his throat than when he had come. That last business, the lettering on the painted-over oval on the wall— it had been so well hidden.

What had Milano been so afraid of?

It was a warning for whoever came after. A warning about what?

CHAPTER 33

It was mid-shift at the Dugout and quiet. Most of the cop-patrons were out in the middle of their evening tours, so Hobbes had the back of the gin mill all to himself.

Gracie put down two beers at his table and went back to sit at the bar with Paul, the Greek restaurateur. She knew when a cop wanted to be left alone, and Hobbes was all over with those vibes.

He had ordered two beers so he could knock one down fast to calm his still-jangled nerves. So he could put behind him the creepy feelings he'd picked up in the basement of the cabin and that had clung to him like a bad smell all the way back to the city.

He had the other beer to sip while he decided whether to be smart about this and turn his back, or stupid and plunge right ahead, wallow in it—try to answer all the whys and what fors that followed him down out of the mountains.

You sit in a bar, you drink, you try to forget. But it never works. Fate won't allow it.

You know it in your bones: The thing you can't see is too big for you, too scary, too much.

That's the test.

Or so I tell myself.

*I tell myself that at that moment, strong people move
forward. Anyway.*
No matter what it is that they'll find.

Hobbes had the jump-in-with-both-feet choice
piled on the table in front of him: some of Milano's
books and monographs. *The Dictionary of Angels: Including the Fallen Angels, The History and Practice of
Magic, Grimoire of Honorius, The Magus, Kabbalah De-
nudata, Essentials of Demonology, Parvi Lucii Libellus de
Mirabilus Naturae Arcanis.*

Leave this whole Milano thing where it is, part of
Hobbes kept saying. Just immerse yourself in standard police procedure—witnesses, physical evidence,
tips, leads, forensics—and solve the Muskavich-
Noons murders the conventional slog-it-out way.

Ignore the Reese mind-fucks. Surely, they were
over now. Done. The man was dead and buried,
after all.

The other part of him said: Don't be a wuss, these
are just books, open 'em, find out what "Azazel"
means at least, maybe there's some kind of weird
surprise in store.

A slippery slope, anything even hinting of the su-
pernatural, Hobbes knew. He'd seen other cops bite
on the lure of psychics and clairvoyants and get
burned; embarrass themselves and the force; get
conned, do something stupid.

He sat staring at an old leather-bound book enti-
tled *Fallen Angels.* He dove in. What the hell, he had
half a lifetime of evidentiary training behind him; he
wasn't going to suddenly go all soft in the head from
reading a couple of books of mythology.

He took up the book and read a page here, a page
there. He was on his fourth beer when his eyes

slowed on a paragraph that named, among the more heinous and powerful creatures of the wilderness and the ancient world, the demon Azazel.

Seven serpent heads, fourteen faces, twelve wings. Lord of Hell, Seducer of Mankind.

Okay. Azazel a demon. Listed here among those demons who passed among men and wielded their influence directly. Then Hobbes's eyes froze on a line of text: "These demons pass by touch."

Hobbes stared at the line. He mouthed it: "These demons pass by touch."

A thought arced through his brain, but it was not the kind of thought a man of Hobbes's intellectual habits could ever credit. The thought had to do with Gretta Milano saying, "Did he touch you or grab you?"; with the image of Reese reaching through the bars, squeezing his hand, reacting; saying, "Still a good boy."

Hobbes dismissed the idea as fast as he thought it. Dismissed it as subversive to any sane man's basic and primary drive to corral the chaos of the world within a coherent, explainable order. The ideas filling these books of magic and mythology in front of him were anathema to the Hobbesian credo: "Figure out what the hell was really going on." Deal in hard, verifiable facts. Forget every other kind of bullshit.

Enough.

He shook himself out of it.

He knocked back his fourth beer, piled up his books and said good-bye to demons. He waved to Dick the bartender on his way to the door.

Hobbes blew out of the bar and walked toward his car parked a couple of long blocks down.

When I want to think, I walk.

He took his time, crossing the street, passing under the elevated train tracks. The pattern of lights and his solitary figure made a stark and beautiful image.

I like the night. The streets. Smells. The sense of another world.

It was a trick he used when he knew he'd be drinking. Give yourself a good walk before you get in the car and drive. The trick of a careful man.

Sometimes it's a world all your own. You're the only one out there—intimate acquaintance of the dark.
You feel calm, relaxed. You feel you could outwalk the most distant city lights.

Hobbes passed into a dim area between widely spaced street lamps, walking beside a high wall that made his steps bounce and echo off the tall, blank-faced warehouse opposite.

He blinked. His face changed, snapping from reverie to alert.

Did you ever feel—sometimes you don't even know until afterwards—like you were being watched?

Footsteps.
Hobbes walked a few more steps. Confirmed it: Someone was following him.

Sometimes you come face-to-face with yourself. Right. Another version of you.

Hobbes glanced over his shoulder.
Saw no one.

He walked a few steps more. Puzzled. Then quickly stopped and turned again, looked.

Still no one in sight. The footsteps had stopped, too.

Hobbes resumed walking. The footsteps resumed.

He had a powerful spooky sense that he was being followed by something *invisible*. How else to say it?

He walked slower . . . coming to a decision. He couldn't run. He must face it.

He stopped, whirled, ran back toward the footsteps. Burdened by his armload of Milano's books, he sprinted down the street, looking in every direction. Every dark building, every doorway, every parked car.

Nothing was visible, no sign of anyone. He owned the street.

And he was going buggy.

Then, as he turned around, exasperated, something flashed through the corner of his vision.

Footsteps? Running up the steel-and-concrete stairs to the elevated subway station.

Hobbes sprinted to the three-tiered stairs, swung around the bronze newel post and ran up them two at a time. A man in athletic shape, chasing something that needed chasing.

What?

At the top he came out on the platform. It was empty. He could see the rear lights of a train that had pulled out thirty seconds earlier. It was already a good ways down the track. Whoever Hobbes was chasing could not have made that train.

He walked a few steps to make certain no one was there, lurking behind an advertising kiosk, hunched in a recess.

He shook his head, aggravated and spooked. He turned back toward the stairs.

And as he did, a shadow moved on the platform across the tracks.

Hobbes glanced over as he was walking, saw nothing. Stopped, stared. Nobody.

He loped down the stairs toward the street.

On the opposing platform the shadow of whoever was following Hobbes, whoever was watching, moved a little ways out from behind a pillar. Just the shadow, no substance.

A train came screeching into the station on that side, and when it pulled away and clattered on down the tracks, Mouse Face, the fat-bellied GM worker, was on it, smirking, staring straight ahead.

CHAPTER 34

A crisp, clear, sunny day. The kind of day that said the idea of lurking evil was a figment. Hobbes drove down the leafy residential street feeling absurd. As if he were turning into some kind of superstitious flake.

He pulled into a parking place across from Gretta Milano's apartment building. What was he going to say? What was real enough to talk about? And what did he expect her to say or do?—coming here as he was, against her express wishes, to spout nonsense.

He was just getting out of his car when Gretta exited her apartment. He moved quickly and intercepted her, fell in step.

"I went to your family's place in the mountains," he blurted. To heck with small talk; he didn't know how long he'd have with her before she gave him the bum's rush again.

Gretta showed no surprise at seeing him—in fact, no reaction at all. She just kept walking. "Beautiful, isn't it?" she said, glancing at him neutrally. "The trees, the water . . ."

"Yes, beautiful. What's 'Azazel' mean?" Hobbes said without transition. "Your father wrote it on the basement wall and painted it over. His dictionary says it's the 'evil spirit of the wilderness'." He gave a very skeptical laugh. "Whatever that is."

She walked on in thoughtful silence, giving him a sidelong look as though debating whether to answer at all.

"Some of the other books your dad had up there talk about 'demons,'" Hobbes said. "What *is* this?" He laughed again, threw his hands out, I-don't-get-it.

Gretta reached her car, opened the door, turned and looked at him. "Walk away," she said. Not mean, just advising. With the weight of authority behind it.

Hobbes reacted to that, taken aback by the sheer abruptness.

Gretta got in her car and closed the door. She rolled down the window and said, "If you enjoy your life, if there's even one human being you care about, give this case to someone else."

He looked at her with a wry smile of disbelief. "I can't do that, Miss Milano," he said unhesitatingly. "This is my job."

She nodded slowly. As if accepting the deeper meaning of his words. Almost as if approving.

She started the car and drove away.

Hobbes went back and sat in his car for a long time sweating, literally. He realized now he had desperately wanted her to debunk the whole demon thing, to poo-poo her father's mythical, mystical obsessions. Wanted her to laugh and let him know her father was around the bend on "evil spirits of the wilderness."

Instead, she had given him one very scary warning. She had leant credence to the incredible.

He felt physically ill. The ground was turning to Jell-O under him.

CHAPTER 35

The squad room felt claustrophobic to Hobbes, over-laden with useless papers, memos, files. With meaningless sound and motion. Whereas the salient facts were out there in the street somewhere, or in yet another sordid anonymous apartment of death, or off in the remote mountains.

Denise handed a fax to Jonesy as he came in the door. He stared at it as he ambled toward his desk.

Tacked to the wall behind his and Hobbes's adjoining desks were photos of Muskavich and Noons, and of their desecrated apartments. Hobbes stood close, examining the crime-scene photos, looking for something that might hint at what the hell was going on.

Stanton came up to Hobbes and handed him some papers.

"What's this?" Hobbes asked.

"Phone company sent muds and luds for Noons's and Muskavich's apartments," Stanton said.

As Hobbes examined the records, Stanton pointed casually to one line on each bill that was underlined or highlighted. "See these calls here?" he said. "They were made right around the time each guy got killed. Give or take."

"You mean . . . the killer phoned my apartment?"

"Sure looks like it," Stanton said.

Hobbes thought about that. "Stanton," he said, "you know Reese used to call me all hours."

"Reese is dead," Stanton said flatly.

"Yeah," Hobbes said, "but whoever's doing this was in league with Reese or is imitating Reese—and he's still calling me. Here. At home. I mean how many times do I have to change my number?"

Stanton, his tone still casual and friendly, said, "The more you change it, the more it looks like someone on the inside."

"Like a cop?" Hobbes said.

"Yeah," Stanton said. He gave Hobbes a friendly cuff. "Hey, it's nothin' to me, but the egos upstairs . . ." He meant Hobbes was one of their own, they'd have to answer for him, see the mess in the papers, get egg on their faces. . . . "*I* know you, they don't know you," Stanton said. "You hear what I'm saying?"

"With both ears," Hobbes said.

Stanton nodded and headed off.

Hobbes stared after him.

Hobbes grumbled to his partner as he walked up, "I'm startin' to lose my sense of humor." He saw Jonesy's expression. "Whatchoo got?"

Jonesy waved the paper. "Translation came in on the Aramaic," he said. "Whattaya make of *this* shinola?"

He handed the fax to Hobbes and gave a mocking commentary as Hobbes scanned down the page.

" 'I can't enter you by touch'?" Jonesy said, quoting from the fax. "What *is* that? 'I'll fuck you up and down, left and right'— That's in the Bible," he said to be funny. " 'And if that doesn't work, I have other ways'? I don't know. We need a translation on the translation, man."

Hobbes read the material with sweat suddenly seeping around his hairline, feeling cold. He nodded stiffly. "Say that again," he said.

CHAPTER 36

Outwardly, the scene in Hobbes's apartment could not have been more placidly domestic. A quiet evening at home, a time to knit the raveled sleeve of care.

In the living room Art and Sam were playing a game of Mancala, the ancient Egyptian board game of glass pebbles moved around a series of cups in paired rows. They were exchanging occasional laughs and exclamations. It was a game at which Art, despite his handicap, had a kind of savant's facility, and Sam could not beat him no matter how hard he tried.

Nearby in the kitchen Hobbes's activity gave the lie to domestic tranquility.

He sat at the table with all of Milano's books spread out. He had been poring over the strange texts for several hours, and his studies had not relieved his anxious state of mind.

He sat back. Thought. Sipped coffee. Tried to pinpoint the source of what was disturbing him so much in all this.

Reese's mind fuck. It was not like him to give in to mind games. Lou at the precinct tried to work them all the time. Hobbes was immune. Too centered in his own personality, too focused on the nuts and bolts of everyday police work. He just did not have a neurotic streak.

Until now, he thought to himself.

He pulled two books toward him to reread.

"They are not to be recognized," read a line he had highlighted in one of the books.

In the other one he reread the line: "Once inside, they know you and remember. Therefore: they speak all the tongues of Babel."

Hobbes shook his head in disbelief, but he was thinking about something. Something he'd better do. A little insurance policy.

Hobbes moved across the leafy grounds of the university campus. His long stride indicated this was no nostalgic stroll revisiting ye college days of yore. He had a purpose.

He approached a gray Gothic stone building constructed a hundred years before, the kind of hideous, gloomy pile that exists only on college campuses and in horror movies. By nice contrast, the ugly building was disgorging a tide of handsome, fresh-faced students barely out of their teens.

Hobbes stood and watched, struck by the contrast between the vital optimistic human scene and the crabbed, twisted, paranoid motive behind his mission here.

Professor Louders emerged from the building surrounded by students. As he drew near where Hobbes waited, he was proclaiming with great energy to one of his charges.

"It's deceptive," Hobbes heard him say. "The cadence, you see, the cadence is similar, but the linguistic patterns are totally distinct." He stopped, surprised to see Hobbes. "*Alors! Quel* coincidence!"

he said. "Oh, *mon Dieu.* Well now. You got my fax,
I suppose?"

"I sure did," Hobbes said, walking with him. "It
was very provocative."

Exactly the right thing to say to the professor.
What could be more delightful to an academic than
to be deemed provocative. "I certainly thought so!"
Louders said with a huge grin. "I assume it's from
some ancient text—except for some of the more color-
ful language—but I've been unable to locate anything similar."

"Please," Hobbes said. "Don't bother yourself. I'm
actually here—"

Louders turned to him eagerly. "Don't tell me you
have another one?" he said. "They're great fun,
actually."

"Not quite," Hobbes said. "I want you to teach me
how to say something."

"Oh," Louders said. "Oh good! In what
language?"

CHAPTER 37

Hobbes watched the tape of Reese on the monitor in the precinct video room, ready with the fax of Louders's translation of the Aramaic in his hands.

Unspooling on the video screen was the scene of Reese jutting his hand through the bars toward Hobbes in his weirdly aggressive manner; Hobbes hesitating, then shaking hands.

The instant their hands touched, Reese tilted his head and looked hard into Hobbes's eyes as though in recognition. "Still a good boy," he said, and tried to caress Hobbes's hand in a strange way.

Hobbes watched himself yanking his hand away, saying, "Hey, I'm not your priest."

"Sure you are," Reese said.

Then suddenly Reese was into the strange tongue, muttering in nonsense syllables, staccato, unintelligible. The no-longer-spoken, biblical subdialect of Syrian Aramaic.

Hobbes read along on the fax, hearing the professor's voice in translation in his head. "I can't enter you by touch," Louders's translation said. Reese went on in his rapid-fire gibberish, and Hobbes read the translation: "But even when I *can* get inside you, after I'm spirit, I *won't* . . ."

Hobbes watched intently. Okay, that was the English, but even in English it was incomprehensible. What the hell did it mean? He grimaced. He flicked the paper in irritation. "After I'm spirit . . . when I *can* get inside you . . ." What horse manure.

From above and to one side in the video room—while Hobbes shook his head and muttered, talking back to the clown on the tape—eyes were watching Hobbes himself.

"No," Reese's taped voice—and with it Louders's in translation—continued, "better I get *you* for real. I'll fuck you up and down, left and right, coming and going. . . ."

The watcher pulled back slightly. Then rubbed against the glass of the small, high window that looked down into the precinct.

A cat.

It perched on the windowsill, watching Hobbes. It jumped down from the window, jogged along the alley toward the front of the building.

". . . left and right, coming and going," the two voices in Hobbes's head said. "I'll get so close to you . . . so close it breaks you. And if that doesn't work? Well . . . I have other ways. I have so many many ways."

Hobbes was about to see one.

The cat padded around the building until it reached the front entrance to the precinct. It sprinted up the steps and rubbed against a cabdriver who had paused by the door to crush his cigarette.

CHAPTER 38

The cabdriver, a wide-bodied middle-aged cigar-chewer, pushed through the heavy wooden doors and entered. He trudged across the floor toward the front desk.

At the same moment Hobbes came out of the video room and headed for the front desk.

The cabdriver reached into his jacket pocket as he moved. His elbow akimbo, he pulled out a piece of paper with some writing on it, and the elbow lightly brushed against a lanky, blond-mustached detective, Joe.

The taxi driver walked on to the desk and plunked down the piece of paper. "Yeah, you're releasing a Richard Suckle," he said to the duty officer. "He called for a cab."

Hobbes picked up a manila envelope with his name on it from a corner of the desk and headed back toward the squad room.

Joe, the detective, crossed toward the stairs, passing Tiffany just coming in. He touched her arm. "Hey, Tiff," he said, "looking cute today."

Tiffany nodded thanks—What got into him?—and headed back toward the squad room.

She walked into the squad room and veered

toward Denise, who was standing at her own desk, holding up a file of papers in her direction.

"Rap sheet on Bobby Stiggers," Denise said.

Their hands touched as Tiffany took the file. Denise immediately looked around, picked up another file and crossed the room to Lou's desk. She lifted up Lou's big hand with her left hand and plopped the file in it with her right, looking at him.

Lou stared at her, watched her walk away, then stood up.

We go along, and we're sure we have a pretty sound grasp of reality. Then we feel a door open somewhere.

We know with a chilling certainty there are other levels.

Lou stared after Tiffany and stood up and looked over at Hobbes. He picked up some plastic sandwich wrap off his desk, stood, went over to Hobbes's desk and half sat on it.

"Hey, Hobbes," he said, "can you tell me something?"

Hobbes looked up: "Shoot."

Lou leaned across the desk in an oddly dominant posture and lowered his voice. "The other day, in the basement?" he said. "You were reading an old file."

For one long instant Lou seemed physically threatening to Hobbes. Was he about to leap over the desk and attack him?"

"What about it?" Hobbes said.

Lou's hand inched across Hobbes's desk. "Well," Lou said, "it looked like you had some kind of map there."

While Hobbes looked at Lou's face, Lou was picking up Hobbes's pen with the plastic wrapping.

Lou went on: "Did you go someplace?"

Hobbes was wary. What was this line of questioning about? "Yeah," he said. "Out in the country."

Lou got off the desk and stood up. "It's great to
get out of town, isn't it?" he said.

"Uh-huh," Hobbes said.

Lou smiled. "I used to go to a house up in the
mountains," he said, "sit by the water. Man, it was
beautiful."

Hobbes barely nodded, impatient, waiting for the
game to play itself out.

Out of Hobbes's line of sight, Lou folded the pen
in his hand. "I'm curious, though," he said.
"Where'd you go?"

Hobbes stared at him.

Lou smiled. He was backing away from the desk.

Hobbes flashed on something. What? Something in
Lou's manner. Couldn't pin it down. "Why do you
ask, Lou?" he said.

Lou's smile became overt, mocking . . . and to
Hobbes's astonishment he started to sing. Under his
breath, just for Hobbes:

"Time . . . is on my side . . . Yes, it is . . ."

Hobbes stared at him. Freak-y. Hobbes was
stunned. How did he—?

At that moment Lou backed into Lawrence, their
hands touching, and the pen, wrapped in plastic,
passing from one man to the other, out of Hobbes's
sight.

The song moved, too.

"Time . . ." Lou started.

". . . is on my side, Yes it is," Lawrence finished.

Hobbes knew he was watching something weird.

As Lawrence walked away, he bumped into a
young black cop named Mike. Hobbes saw the
change in both of them after they touched.

And the song passed again.

Mike sang: "I'll come runnin' back . . . I'll come runnin' back . . ."

Hobbes jumped up as Mike headed out the squad room doorway toward the front desk. "Hey, Mike," he said.

Mike gave Hobbes a casual, brazen look—and kept on, past the door.

Hobbes moved quickly after him.

CHAPTER 39

Hobbes rushed out of the squad room, looked toward the street door: no Mike.

He turned. There was Mike standing behind the main desk. Hobbes walked over to him. "Hey Mike," he said, "why were you singing that song?"

Mike looked at him, a different attitude than he had shown inside. "Song?" he said. "Was I singing something?"

Hobbes realized that the presence, the influence—even now he couldn't bring himself to call whatever was affecting these people a "demon"—he realized it had left Mike.

Hobbes spun and looked toward the door.

Two people were going out: a gray-coiffed society woman with an expensive handbag and a well-dressed short man, almost a midget. The almost-midget turned back, looked at Hobbes and grinned.

Hobbes sprinted after him.

He burst through the tall wooden doors, took the precinct steps at a run and stopped, looking both ways on the crowded street. Couldn't see any sign of them one way, couldn't see them the other.

Finally, he spotted the almost-midget. "Hey!" he shouted, "hey, you!"

The almost-midget didn't seem to hear. Was he

hurrying away? Hobbes moved after them, shaking his head, frustrated, unsure what to do.

An idea came. This wasn't the way he'd foreseen it, but maybe now was the time—the just-in-case. Now he could use it.

He glared after the almost-midget and shouted, "*Innah yahdah-hahnah d'minnou aht!*"

"I know who you are. I know who you are!"

The almost-midget did not react, but, by his side, walking with him, the gray-coiffed society dame turned her head sharply and stopped.

Hobbes saw it. Their eyes met. A frozen moment.

It was she. And he knew it. The society woman was Azazel.

Hobbes, stunned, muttered, "Holy shit."

The society woman eyed him closely, then took a few sauntering steps toward him. "Syrian Aramaic," she said with an ironic smile. "How clever."

"Thanks," Hobbes said dryly.

Hobbes approached her. She made no movement to flee. Quite the contrary, she looked him in the eye with a thin conceited smile on her face. In her hand was the plastic sandwich wrapping.

Hobbes kept coming. "It's true what I said," he said. "I do know who you are."

She just looked at him defiantly. Challenging, not fully buying his boast.

"Azazel," Hobbes said. He couldn't quite believe he was saying it or buying it himself.

The woman's face shifted, fast like slides. Surprise . . . disbelief . . . fury. Her eyes were small and red. Her voice savage and husky. "Where'd you get that," she said, "from Milano's place?"

Hobbes stared her down.

"Yes," she snarled. "You found something up

there. Well"—her face reddened in quiet rage—
"some things, pal, you shouldn't know."

She reached out and touched the almost-midget.
He turned on Hobbes. "And if you know," he
barked, "you should never ever tell."

The almost-midget spun around and touched a fat
man moving by. The fat man's eyes bored into Hobbes
as he glided past him. "Beware my wrath," he said.
Cold, ruthless.

The fat man turned away, touched someone—a
thin-faced hairdresser. She glanced back at Hobbes
and walked on, veering to touch a bespectacled
Asian student. The student cast a look at Hobbes and
casually touched a lawyer with a bulging briefcase.
The lawyer swiveled for a look at Hobbes as he
moved off.

Hobbes realized that he was watching the demon
leave.

What he didn't see was his pen passing, too. As
the demon moved, each "host" glanced back at
Hobbes. It was an eerie effect, a series of flashing
faces, receding . . .

The flashing stopped; the demon vanished. In a
matter of seconds, Azazel could have been any one
of a hundred people.

Hobbes stood there, stunned. He pondered what
the society woman just said, and he realized with a
cold certainty: He had made a mistake.

CHAPTER 40

Hobbes returned to the precinct and walked into the squad room. He looked at Lou, at Lawrence. They were all going about their business, back to normal. Did they have any remembrance of what had just transpired?

Hobbes walked up to Lou.

Lou looked up at him.

Hobbes stared at him, saying nothing.

"Well?" Lou said.

"What was going on back there?" Hobbes asked.

"Back where?" the big, mustachioed cop said. "Whattaya mean?"

"Before," Hobbes said. "When you were singing."

"Singing?" Lou said. "I wasn't singing. Lawrence was singing, or maybe it was Mike . . . some sixties thing. I hated the fuckin' sixties." He laughed harshly.

Hobbes nodded. Thought. This wasn't working. He walked to his desk, dug out the piece of paper on which he had written Gretta's phone number. He dialed.

While waiting, he wanted to jot something down. He felt around for his pen, a piece of paper. Found the paper, no pen. He called over to Jonesy, "Hey, d'you take my pen? I can never keep stuff on my desk. Where is my pen?" He lifted up papers, looked on the floor under his chair.

His pen at that moment was far away, being handed on yet again, this time to a young actress who was stepping off a bus. She put it and the plastic sandwich wrapping in her purse without thinking and carried it onward.

The phone rang in Gretta's cramped, book-gorged university office.

Plaster-cast and oil-painted angels watched over the space here as they did at Gretta's home. An illustrated medieval scroll with a Latin holy text hung over the door. Sacred objects from a range of traditions—a chalice, a Buddha, a cross, a Jewish tefillin, an ankh—peeked out from between the books on the bookshelves. The place almost had the feel of a religious grotto, not a musty academic lair.

Gretta turned from her computer terminal beneath the Sistine Chapel poster, reached across a pile of student blue books and picked up the phone.

"Hello?"

His voice came quietly over the line. "It's Hobbes," he said. "I saw it. It came here. I need more information, and I need it now."

Gretta sighed to herself, not surprised by the call. She didn't answer right away, thinking about the implications before deciding.

CHAPTER 41

City Hall Plaza was a busy public place to have an intimate, intense conversation.

Standing off at one edge of a giant circular mosaic pavement at the center of the plaza, out of the direct flow of circulating foot traffic, they could talk freely and not be overheard.

They *were* talking openly, animatedly, emotionally. Yet both had the subtle, eerie feeling they were not so anonymous in the crowd as they wished.

"I appreciate your situation, I really do," Hobbes started saying.

He couldn't escape the tight, claustrophobic apprehension that gripped him in waves.

"Your parents are dead; their lives were ruined," he said. "I'm very sorry about that, but I need to know what's going on, okay?" He looked at her with hard pleading. " 'Cause if this thing is what it seems to be, what the books say it is—I mean is this for real?" He couldn't help a skeptical roll of his eyes. "You believe this stuff?"

From a distance someone *was* watching Hobbes and Gretta in this charged moment. The watcher could have moved closer, but did not choose to.

Out of fear of discovery? Or was it out of a preference for working indirectly, for nipping around the edges. Some do their best work unseen. Why risk getting caught out?

And there *was* danger—the danger of putting up defenses even further, of spoiling the game.

". . . Is this for real?" Hobbes was saying. "You believe this stuff?"

Gretta never answered without thinking. "I believe more is hidden than is seen," she said at last.

"You're tellin' me," he said with irony. "Look, I'm trying to get my mind around this. What is happening here? Am I about to die, like your father? Some . . . *thing* just *threatened* me." He glared at the heavens in exasperation. "And Reese! He threatened me in Aramaic! He said if he couldn't get me one way, he'd get me another; what *is* that?"

Gretta nodded calmly, as though none of this was taking her by surprise. "What else did Reese say?" she said.

"No, no," he said hotly. "I'm asking the questions now, and you're answering, see?, 'cause if I don't know what's going on—" He shrugged: I don't have a chance.

Her voice came low, soft, and powerful; surprising. "We're not supposed to know," she said. "We're not supposed to see. Like the Mafia: they don't even exist."

"Okay, good—'they,'" Hobbes said, pacing. "That's a start. But where do *they* come from? What the hell *are* they?"

She stared at him. Still reluctant. He didn't know it, but he was asking a lot of her. A lot.

"Mr. Hobbes," she said. "There are certain phenomena which can only be explained . . . if there is a God. And there are angels." She gave him a beat to get on her wavelength. "Some of these angels were cast down. And a few of the fallen, the most awful and terrifying, were punished by being deprived of form. They can only survive in the bodies of others. Inside human beings . . . they wreak their vengeance."

"Whoa," Hobbes said, raising his hands. He'd asked and he'd gotten much more than he was ready to handle. "My work is based on evidence, facts."

"Mine, too," Gretta said, facing him squarely. "But aren't your facts rather resistant to normal interpretation?"

Hobbes's silence was a kind of acknowledgment.

But he was still deeply, inherently skeptical. "What you're saying," he said, "is that Edgar Reese was actually . . ."

"At the time you knew him, he was . . . not himself," Gretta said.

Hobbes opened his hands: "He was Azazel?"

Gretta nodded. "Yes. Azazel. Sadistic, left-handed, likes to sing."

"Reese," Hobbes said. "Why would he focus on me?"

"Demons are lonely," she said. "They never own, they always rent. So when they find someone who's totally ravaged, they bond, they become attached."

"You're saying I provoked him by catching . . . his host? Reese?"

"You got his attention," Gretta said. "After all, you do a lot of good work for the other side. So he tried to get inside you—remember? He shook your hand? But that didn't work, you're too spiritually strong. So now he'll try to get you some other way."

Hobbes eyes went a little wider. "That's what he

did to your father?" he said quietly. "The planted evidence, the frame-up, the murders."

She nodded. And fell silent, watching him.

"Well," Hobbes said, "what do we do? How do you fight them? Is it even possible?"

"I believe so," Gretta said. "And I'm not alone. There's a network of people. I don't even know who they are. I have secret phone numbers. Stockholm, New Delhi." She looked at him almost apologetically, knowing it all sounded incredible. "None of us has more than two phone numbers, so if one person goes under, he or she can't take down the whole network."

Hobbes gaped. "These people think it's possible to . . ."

"We know that God limited demons and made them mortal," Gretta said. "And He put a few of us here to fight them. Nobody knows how many. Thirty-six in each generation, according to ancient Judaic lore. The *Lamed Vav* they're called in Hebrew. The Thirty-six."

Hobbes stared at her, incredulous. "A few of *'us'*? Who? Who us? Us who?" he said. "You're not saying . . . ? Wait a minute. You don't think I'm one of these . . ."

Gretta shrugged and said very carefully, "Maybe, maybe not." Then she quoted him back to himself: "You're just doing your job."

"Yeah, right," Hobbes said. Little did he know. "Okay," he said, back to the practical business. "You said God limited these things and made them mortal. I won't ask you how you know that, but that must mean they can be killed?"

"By the right person," she said.

"And who is that?" Hobbes said. "What does that mean?"

"This is religion, Mr. Hobbes," she said. "We're dealing with matters of fate, divine order. The right man—"

"Or woman," Hobbes said.

"Yes—exactly," she said.

"So it could be me," Hobbes said, "it could be you, it could be anyone."

Gretta nodded. "The right person, of the right character, with the right knowledge . . ."

He stared at her . . . realizing. "This is what you . . . You've been preparing to do this."

She flashed him a look: unmasked.

"Can I ask you something personal?" he said.

"Everything is personal if you're a person," she said.

"Is this why you live alone?"

"Well, there's a difference," she said. "Between risking for yourself and for someone else."

"Go on," he said, knowing exactly what she was talking about.

She shot him a look. These questions crossed a personal line, and she had to decide then whether to confide in him or not.

She took the step. "If I had someone," she said, "I'd want to share: my life, thoughts, my work. But if I shared this, I'd put them at risk. I don't have a right to do that."

"You can talk to me," Hobbes said. Her look made him hasten to add, "I don't mean you have to. I don't mean there's anything else to it. Just: you can if you want to."

She stared at him. "That's a very nice thing to

say," she said. "Or else it's the sliest come-on I've ever heard."

He stared back, without expression. "Thank you," he said.

She laughed.

"Either way," he said, "I mean—" What he meant was, it was kind of a compliment, wasn't it? But the moment had already gotten too complicated.

Another laugh from Gretta.

"I better go," she said. "I have a twelve o'clock class."

A nod. A smile. A warm good-bye. And a shiver against the cold. They parted, took off in opposite directions.

After a few steps Gretta glanced back after Hobbes. A little secret smile of pleasure.

The watcher across the plaza saw them split up and go in different directions. A moment's hesitation, and then the watcher made up his mind.

CHAPTER 42

On one side of the street, the form of Gretta walking. Followed by several others, ordinary pedestrians. But nobody following her.

From the other side of the street came an older man who fell into step with the others behind Gretta. Slicked-back gray hair down the back of his neck, gaudy purple patterned tie, dark raincoat. This man walked purposefully, staring at Gretta's back.

Unaware, Gretta strode briskly along the crowded commercial thoroughfare rubbing her hands together against the chill. The stalker closed ground, step by long step, and extended his arm to touch her. A foot away, six inches . . .

Gretta, sensing something, turned and glanced in an electronics store window, and saw the gray-haired man's reflection, his reaching arm.

She gasped, spun away to the side. Trapped in the store vestibule, she backed up to the glass.

"I'm sorry," the man said. "I was just going to tap you on the shoulder."

Gretta stared at him with blank-faced anxiety.

"You're a friend of John Hobbes, aren't you?" the man said, smiling. "I'm Jay Reynolds." He held out his hand to shake.

The hand hung in the air. Gretta stared at him, refusing to take it, refusing his touch.

The man lowered his hand and his expression changed. "So you know," he said. "How lovely." He took a half step toward her, eyeing her intently. "You're not just Hobbes's chippie, are you? Do I know you?" He stared at her with a "you seem oddly familiar" look.

Paralyzed, Gretta flattened herself against the far glass wall, caged, cornered by this creature who struck deep fear in her.

The stalker moved closer, gave a playful pout: "Come on, tell me." His tone hardened. "I'm about to find out anyway."

Smiling at her silence, her suppressed panic, he started to raise his arm toward her. "I love it when people know," he said. "Before I touch them?" His arm came up ever so slowly. "It's like foreplay." His hand six inches from her face . . .

A rough-trade street kid in a gangsta leather jacket pushed between them, heading into the store.

Gretta bolted out of the vestibule, down the street, running for all she was worth.

The stalker sprinted after her, but crashed into the first kid's gangsta pal, also trying to get into the store. They fell, rolled together.

Gretta spied salvation: a businessman getting out of a cab. She ran toward the cab in all-out terror.

On the pavement, the second gangsta kid rudely shoved the gray-haired man off him—shoved him with a rancor that told: the demon had passed.

At the cab, Gretta looked back. She saw the gray-haired man and the kid on the ground. The older man looked dazed. A bolt of relief shot through her.

What she didn't see was the kid staring at her,

enraged. Nor did she see the kid reach out and grab the ankle of a topcoated pedestrian.

The pedestrian's arm shot up and touched the woman just ahead of him.

Something made Gretta turn and look again, just in time to see that woman's arm move, touch the person ahead, and his arm go up and touch another. Like dominos falling, one after another, pedestrians reaching, touching, sending the evil along. The demon flew through the crowd toward Gretta.

Seeing, not quite comprehending, she felt a cold fear coil around her like a boa. It was washing toward her, a human-born wave of terror. Horrified, she finally realized what was happening.

She leapt into the cab and slammed the door.

Just then a middle-aged man with benign face and opaque, malignant eyes slapped his hand on the window. He reached for the door handle. Gretta sprang for the lock, pawing it down. She got there first. *Click.* Locked. She won.

"Drive!" she said to the cabbie.

The man swung his free hand—*Smash!* And shattered the cab window, spraying chiclets of safety glass all over the backseat.

He lunged through the window at Gretta. She threw herself back. His hand stopped inches from her face.

"Go! Go! Go!" she screamed. The groping hand strained toward her. The driver hit the gas.

The demon's hand loomed before Gretta's face, then floated backward out the window, a ghostly image. The man crashed to the ground and rolled.

Inside the cab, Gretta gasped in relief, tried to still her heart. Escape. Safety.

The driver looked over his shoulder. "Lady," he said, "you're payin' for that window, huh?"

CHAPTER 43

The high-vaulted ceiling of one of God's houses.

Gretta was staring up into the majestic crown of a cathedral-style Gothic church, one of humankind's attempts to celebrate in towering arches and domes the grandeur and grace of the Lord. Gretta sought such a roof over her head often: to elevate the soul and seek refuge from the fear that dogged her every day.

She sat hugging herself in a pew, gazing up at the candles, the crucifix, the angels in the friezes and the stained glass. Always before she had been able to find solace in the religious iconography: evocative, beautiful, yet strange and frightening.

But now, this evening—the church empty except for Gretta waiting—she failed to find it. She was afraid even here.

Hobbes entered at the back and walked down the aisle toward her.

Gretta had called him as soon after it happened as she could get to a safe phone. Not from her home. She had that little margin of safety; her home wasn't known or connected to Hobbes in any way.

As he slid in next to her, she exclaimed in self-loathing, "I ran. He came after me and I ran."

"You weren't ready," Hobbes said.

"That's the point," she said. "You have to be ready." She gave a sad, ironic smile. "You know what it is? I never believed this day would come. I thought God'd make it up to me, I'd be a good girl, and God would show me an angel instead." She hated herself for her naivete, for the sheer irrelevance of her emotions and thoughts. "I always wondered if they really have wings."

Hobbes gave a half smile of understanding. "Does he know who you are?" he asked.

She shook her head.

"Then we can't be seen together," he said. "Not anymore."

She nodded slowly. Of course he was right.

They both felt the disappointment.

Two figures alone, lit by candles, in this empty, echoing House of God. She had gone for so many years by herself, with only the few phone numbers, the short, anonymous conversations across continents and oceans. This was the first time she'd been able to sit face-to-face with another human being and talk about this frightening stuff.

Maybe she—and Hobbes—*were* among the thirty-six righteous souls of their generation. Maybe they *were Lamed Vavniks.* There was consolation and strength in that thought.

But also great weight. Gretta could not but take the possibility seriously; and along with it, the sense of a terrible responsibility. The legend said, it was on these few do-gooders' account that the life of the world was continued; that the Lord did not simply step back from the vale of evil and let it descend to utter wrack and ruin.

How could she not take up the standard and fight the fight?

But how could she do it alone?

Please don't make me go it alone anymore, she cried out in her head. But she clamped her teeth tight to prevent the words from escaping from her mouth. She looked up at all the marble and stained-glass guardian angels and willed strength into her bones.

CHAPTER 44

Hobbes stuck his head in the doorway of Stanton's office. The lieutenant sat behind his desk, drinking his morning coffee and reading the overnight reports.

"You wanted me?" Hobbes asked.

"Yeah, yeah, come in," Stanton said.

Hobbes entered. He pulled a quarter from his pocket as he sat down opposite Stanton's desk. He unconsciously fiddled with the coin.

"So," Stanton said, leaning back. "These murders got you wound up?"

"Bag the chocolates, Stanton," Hobbes said with an ironic look. "What's goin' on?"

"Where were you when Muskavich and Noons got killed?" Stanton said.

Hobbes was incredulous. "Where was I?" he said, half amused. "What, I'm a suspect?"

"Not to me you're not, but . . ."

Hobbes was no longer even half amused. "What is this," he said, "the phone records again? I committed the murders and then called my own apartment?!"

"There's something else," Stanton said. "Prints."

Hobbes looked at him askance: "My prints?"

Stanton stared, expressionless.

"On what?" Hobbes said.

Stanton looked at Hobbes's hands.

Hobbes looked down himself, and opened his palm: a quarter. "On a quarter?" he said. "You found a coin with my prints. . . . You're kidding. Where did you . . . ?"

"Noons's place," Stanton said.

Hobbes nodded pensively a couple of times, grasping the situation. "So this is a frame-up."

Stanton watched him carefully. "Is it?" he asked.

Hobbes glared. "Come on, Stan," he said. "Somebody coulda got it when I bought something . . . Or they coulda taken it off my desk."

He vividly flashed on his missing pen. It could have been that; it could have been anything he'd handled, anywhere. Then the prints were transferred. It was easy. It was done all the time.

And he knew he was being followed. He'd seen Noons himself on the street near his house.

"Yeah," Stanton said. "We did always say this could be a cop."

Hobbes glared at him. The insinuation was quite obvious.

"Hey," Stanton said. "I'm not stupid, you know? I know you know more than you're saying. So tell me."

Hobbes would never sell Stanton short. He knew that his acute mind was always figuring the angles. And he knew his boss had been observing him for days. He shook his head. "You wouldn't believe it, Stan," he said quietly. "You had to be there, okay?"

Stanton put on his friendly, intimate "confidant" mode. "Come on, try me," he said.

Hobbes eyed him, considering it. Then shook his head. *He* barely believed this stuff, and he'd been living through it. Why should he expect Stanton to simply swallow it. Stanton would think that he'd lost a wheel—or was pretending to have lost a wheel.

"I can tell you this much," Hobbes said. "Remember Robert Milano? Well, this is just what happened to him: he got framed."

Stanton stared at him as if seriously considering this.

A sense of doom washed over Hobbes. He realized Stanton was already speculating about his sanity.

"Take my advice, okay?" Stanton said. "Let it alone a few hours. Go home, be with your family. Take a load off."

The two men looked at each other for a long moment.

Hobbes got up and walked out, fighting to get a full breath. Events were beginning to close in. The pattern was identical. Milano had nailed somebody he shouldn't have; retribution followed. Hobbes nailed Reese; Reese waved Milano's name in front of him like a blueprint: read it and weep.

Hobbes felt a vise beginning to squeeze his chest.

CHAPTER 45

Hobbes did leave the office early. He thought he'd be able to breathe out in the open air. He got in his car and drove. Put in some miles on the beltway out along the river.

It was no better. He still felt trapped, hunted. He caught himself warily watching the cars next to him, behind him.

He whipped down off the expressway and went home.

He parked across the street and walked from his car toward his apartment building.

"Hi, Unc," came the call from one of the big chestnut trees in front of his building.

Hobbes looked up in surprise.

There was Sam up in a crotch of the tree, with Toby on a branch nearby. Sam smiled at Hobbes and gave a jaunty wave.

Hobbes waved back. And slowed for half a second as though disturbed by a thought he couldn't quite articulate. He went on.

He keyed his way into his apartment and forgot the troubling thought, glad to be home.

He heard the shower running. He glanced at the pile of mail and moved down the hall into his room. Everything about his attitude said: the day was over, now he was within his own four walls and could relax.

Here things were ordinary. A relief. Nothing would happen here.

In his bedroom Hobbes took off his jacket and started to unbutton his shirt.

He stopped.

He looked around the room. Something was bothering him; he didn't know what it was. Something was different.

Slowly, his eyes scanned the room. And came to rest on his desk. Just a few items, but they were in disarray. Almost as if they were thrown that way to get his attention.

He walked over to the desk and stared, then realized something. He glanced around: the desk, the shelf, the surrounding floor area. He was looking for something that should have been there.

Hobbes walked out of his room and saw Art moving down the hall in his bathrobe. Art had a towel around his head and was drying his hair, his face.

"Hey, Art," Hobbes said, "you didn't move my address book, did you?"

"What?" Art said.

"Have you seen my address book?" Hobbes said, coming toward him.

Art shook his head, nervously, and tried to move past Hobbes.

Something was strange. Art was holding his towel over his right eye. He was not drying his face, he was covering his eye.

Hobbes stopped Art and gently pulled the towel down. Behind the towel Art had a black eye.

Art blinked, mustering the best face he could. "I fell," he said sheepishly.

Hobbes cocked his head. "What?" he said.

"I fell or something," his brother said.

"Art," Hobbes said, "people don't fall down and get a black eye."

"They don't?"

Hobbes shook his head.

"Oh," Art said. His face worked nervously. "Well . . . something."

"It's okay," Hobbes said, putting a reassuring hand on Art's arm. "Say it."

"Sammy," Art said, pained. "He struck me."

Hobbes blanched. The truth washed over him; not of the punch, of the other thing that almost stopped him outside.

He turned and looked through the window toward the chestnut trees out front. In his mind's eye he did a fast replay of his coming home a few minutes before. Only now he saw things differently.

He walked across the street from his car. Sam called down from the tree, "Hi, Unc." Hobbes recognized now that Sam's tone of voice was slightly mocking.

And when he looked up at Sam, he saw the boy smiling down from the tree, giving a wave, but his smile had a slightly superior, slightly sinister quality.

Sam waved with his left hand. And in his right hand he was holding Hobbes's address book.

Art broke through his remembering. "But he didn't mean to, Johnny," he said. "Really. It was an accident, or . . ." He drifted off lamely.

There's a moment when you realize everything is different. You saw it before, even felt it.

But now it's in your face, laughing at you.
This is the moment you need to just sit. Quietly.

Hobbes was already sprinting toward the apartment door. Now this demon thing had gone too far.

CHAPTER 46

Hobbes tore into the hallway of his apartment building. He turned the corner toward the stairs and bumped right into Sam.

Hobbes grabbed him, yanked him up hard to look him in the eye. Bewilderment and fear bloomed on Sam's face. Hobbes was rough, almost out of control.

"Uncle John?" Sam said.

Hobbes saw immediately that Sam was now clear of the demon. He loosened his grip on the boy, thinking quickly. "Where's Toby?" he said.

"Ahhh . . . Still outside," Sam said. "I guess."

Hobbes gave Sam a reassuring pat and sprinted away down the hall, down the stairs.

He ran out of the building into the late afternoon sunshine. He saw Toby sitting casually on the hood of a car across the street, leafing through Hobbes's address book.

"Leave them alone!" Hobbes shouted.

Toby smiled an easy, arrogant smile, which made Hobbes practically explode with rage. "Leave my family alone!" he screamed at the demon festering within Toby.

"Why?" Toby said in a voice clearly not his own. "You come after me, I come after you and yours."

Enraged, Hobbes sprinted toward him. Toby slid off the car and ran, too, with the agile speed of youth.

Hobbes pounded down the street as fast as he could. Toby was even faster, streaking down the pavement, swerving into the street. He wove recklessly through oncoming cars, dodging in and out with insouciance.

Hobbes watched, alarmed; he slowed.

Cars honked and hit their brakes. The address book fell. Toby was fast, fearless. He veered hard in front of a furniture truck and made it all the way across.

A swarthy man in a dark jacket had stopped to watch Toby's daredevilry. Toby ran near him, lunged, grabbed his arm.

The swarthy man pulled away and moved along a few steps.

Toby stopped to catch his breath. Hobbes caught up, took one look at him and spoke with gentle firmness, like a concerned parent. "Go home, Toby," he said.

Up ahead, the swarthy man in the jacket looked back. Then made a sudden move toward a big American car parked at the curb.

The movement caught Hobbes's eye as the guy pulled open the car door and slid in the front seat.

Hobbes walked toward the car.

Inside the car the swarthy man leaned over and opened the glove compartment and set something on the dash. He ripped open his shirt and hunched over; he was doing something Hobbes couldn't see.

Hobbes slowed, approaching nearer, a little cautiously. What was the man up to?

The swarthy man was working on his chest. Something glinted on the dashboard. Hobbes saw what he had placed there: a pistol.

Hobbes froze. What the hell? The last thing he expected was open violence.

In Hobbes's moment of indecision, the swarthy man leapt out, firing the handgun at him. Hobbes jumped to one side.

The swarthy man kept shooting.

Hobbes dove, rolled between two parked cars, drew his 9mm service automatic from the holster behind his hip.

Silence.

Hobbes got his feet under him and crouched in the gutter behind the fender of a parked car. He was unharmed.

He peeked out and instantly pulled back.

Then looked out again.

The swarthy man was standing in the middle of the city street. His pistol was in his fist, but pointed at the ground. His face was strangely calm.

"What's a matter, pal," the guy called. "You afraid to fight me?"

Hobbes thought hard. What were his choices? If this creature didn't get his way, he was capable of turning the gun on pedestrians in an instant. Better Hobbes than his unsuspecting neighbors.

Hobbes readied himself.

He stepped out from behind the car, his pistol at his side.

Face-to-face. Gunfight on Elm Street.

The swarthy man's face curled into a smile. "I knew you'd come out," the husky, edgy voice said. "I know you, Hobbes. I know who you are." With sneering contempt he spouted: *"Innah yahdah-hahnah d'minnou aht!"*

Hobbes reacted to the Aramaic.

The swarthy man started slowly to raise his gun. Very slowly.

A long suspended moment. Jesus. Innocent by-stander or murderous demon? Hobbes was para-lyzed. Fire at this guy, whoever he was? Take him down the same way he would any thug or psycho pointing a firearm at him.

The swarthy man's gun was rising slowly, inexora-bly. Then the man's arm jerked up, the gun aiming at Hobbes's chest.

Debate over, Hobbes whipped his own gun up and fired. The swarthy man spun, fell heavily to the pave-ment. One knee raised briefly, his head turned side to side once.

He lay still.

Hobbes walked toward the motionless body. He passed his address book lying on the street near the man's feet. He looked down at the guy. A middle-aged, nondescript citizen in a dark winter jacket. A collapsed hunk of flesh that seconds ago was breath-ing, hoping, planning.

And possessed, inhabited, used.

Doomed.

Hobbes squatted, put his hand in front of the man's open mouth: no breath. He sighed with relief; he had killed a man, yes, but he had also killed the demon. Thank God.

Thank God?—

It rose.

Something rose.

Coming up out of the body . . . moving away from the car . . . A fat woman stared in shock at the body, at Hobbes. It hovered over her . . . and moved on. A pretty sixteen-year-old girl had been walking home from the 7-Eleven in the minimall, just another day at her after-school hanging place. She, too, had been staring at the scene in the street, too frightened to move. Or almost too frightened. She stepped forward, unaware of course that *it* was over her head.

And then it plunged into her.

She smiled. Pushed back her hair. Stared brazenly at Hobbes.

He took no notice of her.

He was looking down at the blood of the swarthy man pooling outward on the pavement. He knelt by the man, felt his pulse and watched the dark stain grow. With every inch it spread, he felt the solidity of his own life draining away. All sounds ceased in his head; he stood up quickly, looking at the ground as though it were shifting under him.

Then a single sound: The girl on the sidewalk laughing maliciously.

Hobbes spun toward the sound and looked at her, at the mocking look in her eyes. An icy chill ran through him from head to toe. *No!* It couldn't be. But it was.

"Hey, pal. Wake up, Hobbes," the girl said in a harsh voice. "I'm not that easy to kill."

She took a sauntering step or two toward him and snarled. "When my host dies and I move as spirit, *no* man can resist me." She laughed. "What are you going to do? Arrest me? Strip-search me? What are you going to tell Stanton? Good fuckin' luck. I'd love to hear that one."

She turned and coolly walked away.

Hobbes stared after her in horror and called out, "If it's me you want, why don't you just kill *me*?!"

She turned, surprised he would even ask. Surprised it wasn't obvious, especially to Hobbes. "But

I'm still having fun," she said, feigning hurt feelings. Then, low and vicious, "Aren't *you* still having fun?"

She turned and strode off.

Hobbes stared at her back. He looked down at the body at his feet, and a cold sweat began leaking from every pore in his body. He'd just killed someone. An utterly innocent someone?

As the truth began to pulse in waves to deeper levels of his consciousness, Hobbes went into a kind of overload. He sat down heavily in the street next to the dead man and put a listless hand on his arm. His brain ticked down to a meaningless hum. He could do nothing but wait.

CHAPTER 47

Hobbes sat in the street, stunned. Color had been sucked from his sight, sounds came from a great distance, his mind had gone mercifully blank for what seemed an eon.

Pedestrians gathered to ogle. A few asked questions and gave up when the sitting man gave no sign of hearing them.

By the time the colored lights appeared in the distance and the black-and-whites approached, Hobbes was up walking slowly around the body.

But still out of it. Still not even close to being Hobbes, the guy everybody else could automatically count on to deal with it.

Only when he turned and the revolving light of a patrol car flashed right in his eyes did he start to come to.

Cops swarmed and hung yellow crime scene tape from car to car, light post to light post. An EMT checked the body for signs of life and, finding none, waved the coroner's team in. Forensics flashed their still cameras and looked around, ready to chalk down every bullet mark and empty shell casing they could find on the pavement or in cars, poles, buildings, doors.

A good-sized crowd had gathered, and TV minicams were setting up to film from atop KU-band satellite trucks and other perches behind the yellow tape.

"He was standing in the street yelling at him and shooting at him," a dignified, older black man was telling Lou. Lou was jotting in his notebook as the man spoke. "And finally the officer I guess it is," the man went on, "steps forward and the guy starts to shoot again, and the officer brings him down."

"So there's no question that the dead man fired first?" Lou said.

"No question at all," the witness said. "My wife saw it, too, if you want to ask her."

Hobbes was in a daze.

But Stanton had him off to one side and was forcing him to deal with it.

Stanton was pulled tight as a drum; not a particle of his vaunted ironic humor was visible. "A *schoolteacher*, huh?" he said in disgust. "What am I gonna say? What'm I gonna do? We got a weird situation here. Seems like you're kinda specializing in weird situations, and that itself is getting a little weird, know what I mean?"

He paced away and back again, staring down at the swarthy man's corpse as the techs finished their initial work and drew a sheet over the body.

Hobbes watched, expressionless, a flat-line look behind his eyes.

"We know he fired first," Stanton said. "Witnesses corroborate. But his gun was filled with blanks, okay? And he got the gun out of a stolen car; how 'bout that one?"

"It was a setup," Hobbes said.

"He set it up for you to kill him?" Stanton asked sarcastically. "Suicide by cop?"

Hobbes's expression changed abruptly. "I'll be right back," he said and walked away.

"Hey, where you going?" Stanton called. "I'm talking to you!"

Hobbes moved across the yellow tape toward the crowd. He'd spotted Art and Sam watching from the curb in front of the apartment building. Hobbes marched up to Art.

"What're you doing? Are you nuts?" he said sharply. "Take Sam back to the apartment, lock the doors, lock the windows, don't let anybody in. And I mean *anybody*. You understand me?"

Art nodded gravely.

"Can you remember that?" Hobbes asked.

Art nodded again.

"Then *do* it," Hobbes said. "I'll see you later." He started away.

"Johnny," Art said. "Are you mad at me or something?"

Hobbes stopped and came back. He shook his head no and gently patted his brother's face. "Never, Art," he said. "It'll never happen."

Art smiled.

Hobbes gave Sam a pat on the back. "Now go on," he said, "both of you."

Father and son walked off toward the apartment. Hobbes watched them all the way to the stoop, then turned back toward the body in the street.

Lou and Jonesy had joined Stanton, and Lou was shaking his head in mock disappointment, saying to Jonesy, low, "I hate to see the mighty fall, know what I mean?"

Jonesy gave him a go-fuck-yourself glare. He moved toward the arriving Hobbes.

"Now it's letters," Jonesy said. He bent and pulled

the sheet back and bared the schoolteacher's chest. On it, written in magic marker, were the letters, A-P-O. It was what the swarthy man had been doing hunched over in the car while Hobbes approached.

Stanton was closely watching Hobbes's reaction as Jonesy pulled back the man's shirt and revealed the letters. Jonesy and Stanton exchanged a look.

"I told you, Lieutenant," Jonesy said. "It's a cult. We're dealing with some weird psycho Aramaic reincarnation Satan cult.

"Yeah," Stanton said. "Same old, same old."

"A-P-O?" Hobbes said. "It must be some kinda message."

"The killer's sending a message?" Stanton said skeptically. "Hobbes? This time you *are* the killer."

"Sort of," Hobbes said.

"No fucking 'sort of'!" Stanton said. "No breaks! No benefit of the doubt! We're goin' back to the precinct! Now!"

CHAPTER 48

Cold rain pelting down, a miserable nightcap on a hateful day.

Hobbes was numb, as if he were operating on automatic pilot.

He parked in the lot and entered the precinct through the cop entrance at the side. He walked down the long corridor and across the foyer. It was unusually quiet. Only the night-duty officer was at the front desk. Hobbes nodded and went into the squad room.

He went straight to Stanton's office.

Stanton hung up the phone as Hobbes walked in. "We talked to the schoolteacher's wife," Stanton said. "They got married four months ago, she's pregnant, and he just got a raise. So much for suicide by cop. And you're tellin' me you shot this guy because he stole your address book?"

"Well," Hobbes said tiredly, "he happened to be shooting at me at the time."

They stared at each other for a long moment. A stalemate. Stanton didn't pretend to have this figured out, but that didn't stop him from being damned hot about it.

A knock at the door. Stanton rose to answer it,

saying, "I got four years left. I'm not putting my pension in jeopardy."

He opened the door. It was Lou. They whispered. Something passed between them. Hobbes only heard the end.

"I'm taking off," Lou said.

Stanton nodded and closed the door. He came back to his desk. He sighed. "Your pen," he said.

Hobbes looked at him in silence.

"You lost your pen?" Stanton asked.

More expectant silence from Hobbes.

"Yesterday?" Stanton said. "You were lookin' around for it, right?"

"You found it?" Hobbes said. "Where?"

Stanton put a Ziploc evidence bag on the desk. It contained the pen. "Schoolteacher's pocket," he said. "And the only prints on it are yours."

Hobbes flared. "You gonna charge me with planting evidence against myself?!"

Stanton shook his head in disgust. "The officer-involved-shooting team'll need your weapon," he said.

Hobbes looked at him, not believing this was happening to him.

"I'll get the hearing soon as I can," Stanton said.

Hobbes nodded and stared.

Stanton stared back. He took a deep breath. "People want the world to make sense," he said tiredly. "If the only way the world makes sense is to arrest you, then I'll have to do it." He stood up. "Now get the fuck out of here."

CHAPTER 49

After midnight. Hobbes was exhausted.

The conversation with Stanton was only the last of a series of official conversations about the officer-involved-shooting. Long, aggravating, repetitive conversations. Internal Affairs and the department psychologist, those were normal. The pointed, uninformed questions from the Mayor's Office liaison guy and the deputy commissioner, those were ominous. And disquieting.

Hobbes walked out of Stanton's office into a squad room empty but for Jonesy.

Jonesy sat at his desk, puffing away at a weed.

Hobbes looked at him as he moved across the room toward him: quintessential cop, rumpled, bad eating habits, overweight, cruising for a heart attack. Corrupt yet incorruptible. An oak.

A light flickered in the corner of Hobbes's eye as he crossed the room.

It was the TV, tuned to the news. A report on the citizen-officer confrontation on Elm Street. Hobbes's photograph led the story, with the slash line, WITNESSES BACK UP COP'S STORY.

Hobbes detoured and turned off the TV.

Jonesy gave him a quick glance.

Walking by Jonesy's desk, Hobbes saw a loose cig-

arette. He picked it up and was about to stick it between his lips. Instead, he eyed it, debated, then
tossed it down. He'd quit four years before. Why add
one more failure to the growing list? he thought.

He grabbed a plastic evidence bag from the top of
a file cabinet and sat down at his desk. He pulled
his service 9mm from his holster and took the clip
out of it. He tossed the clip in his top drawer and
put the gun in the plastic bag.

Stanton came out of his office, turned off the light
and walked straight through the squad room and
out.

Jonesy got up from his desk and walked after him.

Hobbes glanced up as he went, then back down at
his chore. He sealed the plastic bag and labeled it
with a magic marker.

Jonesy didn't go out the door after Stanton; he
stopped at the coffee machine. He poured two cups,
sniffed at them, shrugged and walked back. He
dropped off one of the cups on Hobbes's desk and
sat down.

Hobbes nodded his thanks. He pulled open his
middle drawer and found the picture of Marcy he
kept in there. He'd stuck it in there a few weeks after
she left, once he'd convinced himself she was really
gone for good.

That was over two years ago. That he'd made little
effort to replace her in his life made him wonder.
Was he more like Gretta than he thought? Was he
isolating himself subconsciously on purpose, knowing the things he felt he had to do in life were too
hard on other people, too dangerous?

He put the photograph carefully back in the
drawer. He was glad for her sake she was gone—
now. The nightmare he was living was likely only to

deepen, it seemed. He wished there were some way to insulate Art and Sam from it all.

Jonesy looked over at him. "It was a clean shot," he said.

"I know," Hobbes said. "It doesn't help."

Jonesy nodded. Sipped his coffee. Winced at the taste. "Where," he said, "do they buy coffee with dirt in it? Can you tell me that?"

Hobbes said nothing. He went on half-consciously sorting through the junk in his middle drawer, an accumulation from years on the force. Business cards, PBA keychains, letters from appreciative and irate citizens, the stubs from the NBA playoff game he'd taken Sammy and Art to last season; a souvenir shell casing from a bullet meant for his head, deflected by a railing at the last instant. He was lost in this debris, lost in remembering how important his policeman's life was to him.

"You wanna talk," Jonesy said slowly, nodding. Jonesy had a sick feeling about the way things were going. He loved Hobbes. " 'Cause from where I sit," he said, "we seem to be dealin' with something that ain't in the manual."

"Yeah," Hobbes said. He looked up at his longtime partner and friend and threw him a fat one. "Jonesy," he said, "what is the point of life?"

Jonesy's eyes bugged slightly. "The point?"

"Yeah."

"Of life?" Jonesy said.

"Yeah."

"The point is: We catch bad guys," Jonesy said.

"Not good enough," Hobbes said.

Jonesy shrugged, puffed out his cheeks, stared at Hobbes. He was serious, ferchrissake. He was asking for some authentic deep thought.

Hobbes inhaled a bit of Jonesy's cigarette smoke and fought the temptation again. "Okay," he said, "shoot me for talking like this."

"Hey," Jonesy said, "it's two in the morning. You can talk any weird shit you want."

"Good," Hobbes said. " 'Cause . . . What're we *doing* here, man? I mean why do we *exist*, can you tell me that? Us, birds, trees, water? *Anything*? Why is it . . . here?"

Jonesy considered falling back on another quippy cop cop-out. But no, not now. "Could be God, Hobbes," he said.

"Yeah, could be," Hobbes said, "but I have a hard time believing we're part of some huge moral experiment conducted by a being greater than we are. Five billion human beings? We're like ants, man? Do we care what ants do, from a moral standpoint?"

"Ants?" Jonesy said. "No."

"But if there's no God," Hobbes said, "how'd we get here? See what I'm saying? Go back to the beginning, the very beginning of time, the big bang or whatever you wanna call it."

"Okay, I'm with you," Jonesy said. "The beginning."

"Right," Hobbes said. "Now what came before?"

"Nothing," Jonesy said, feigning irritation. "It's the beginning."

"No, no, sorry," Hobbes said. "Something as big as the universe does not just *appear* out of nowhere. Some*body* or *thing* had to start it. It's like: Even if there *is* a God . . . who made God?"

Jonesy looked at him askance. "I'm followin' you Hobbes," he said, "but I'm losin' you at the same time."

"I know," Hobbes said, "I know."

"Are we headed somewheres here?" Jonesy said. "Or—"

"That's what I'm asking *you*," Hobbes said. "If there's a purpose to life, we better figure it out."

"Maybe you figure it out, you die," Jonesy said with a snap of the fingers. "Heart attack, stroke. Like: If you know what's what, you aren't allowed to stick around anymore. You get promoted."

Hobbes nodded. Jonesy was making a kind of sense. Knowledge of the kind he was talking about was a little heavy for a person to be carrying around for long. Probably of a nature mere mortals weren't equipped to handle.

"Meanwhile," Jonesy said, "Dolores says we're here to do one thing."

"One thing?" Hobbes asked. "What is it?"

"Different," Jonesy said. "It's different for everybody. Hers is lasagna."

"*One* thing," Hobbes said, "not two."

"Maybe two, I don't know," Jonesy said. "It's just her opinion, Hobbes. It's like: A moment comes, you either do the right thing or the wrong."

That struck a chord. Hobbes thought for a beat, then said, "How do we know when the moment comes?"

Hobbes's phone rang.

They both looked at each other and let out big laughs. When your moment comes . . .

It rang again.

"Like, this could be it for me, huh?" Hobbes said.

"There's the beauty, Hobbes," Jonesy said. "You never know."

Hobbes looked at the ringing phone, back at Jonesy, then picked it up. "Yeah," he said very low. Nothing. *"Hello?"*

He shook his head in irritation, thinking it was another of the Reese/Noons/demon silent calls. He was about to hang up when a voice came across the line.

"John, is that you?" a feminine voice said. "It's Gretta. I just . . . I wanted to see if you're okay."

"Not really," Hobbes said. He glanced at Jonesy. "I'll call you back, okay?" He hung up straightaway, wanting at all costs to protect Gretta's separation and anonymity.

Jonesy was looking at him.

"That was the killer," Hobbes said, deadpan. "We're arranging things."

Jonesy laughed.

Hobbes stood up, put his bagged gun in his desk drawer and locked it. "I'm goin' home," he said.

"Take the weekend off, huh," Jonesy said with a smile. "It's on me."

Hobbes nodded and headed out.

Jonesy looked after him, worried. Wishing he knew what the hell Hobbes was keeping from him in all this. Wishing he could help.

Thinking: How do things just spin out of control sometimes, no matter how good a cop you are? No matter how good a man you are?

CHAPTER 50

Hobbes stepped into his apartment, turned and double-locked the door behind him.

He moved down the hall into the living room, checking to see the windows were locked. He looked in on Art and Sam. They were sleeping peacefully in the same bed. He surveilled the kitchen and other rooms to see if there was anything odd or out of place. He found nothing.

Still, he found no sense of safety or peace. His home had been violated once; it could be again.

He took off his jacket and opened a beer and wandered the length of the apartment and back again.

For any normal kind of trouble he would have told himself: Nail down the problem, figure out a plan, work your way through it. But this? He felt encircled, powerless. What resources did you bring to bear on something that you couldn't see? Something that moved at will from person to person and killed at will. That seemed to be acting purposefully, but according to a logic only it knew.

He spread Milano's books out on the desk in his bedroom and dove into them, looking for *something*.

He read: "The rider on the serpent," said *The Zohar*, describing "the evil Azazel." Chief of the *bene elim* or lower angels, "men spirits."

"Lord of hell, seducer of mankind," another book said.

And another: "That fallen and mighty angel," "a son of fire," "Satan's standard bearer."

Useless stuff. Useless, moaned Hobbes.

In *Enoch I*, he found Azazel characterized as one of the chiefs of the two hundred fallen angels, a third of the heavenly host. It was Azazel, it said, who initiated mankind in the art of making swords and shields. It was he also who taught women to gild their eyes and drape their bodies in finery.

At one time the revered god of the flocks, Azazel was "the first star which fell," and was demoted to the level of demon, according to *The Significance of Satan in New Testament Demonology*.

This is insane! Hobbes thought: demons, fallen angels, men spirits. He was just not a believer. None of it was real.

And yet he'd seen it all; he was in the grip of something that was sure as hell demonic.

Look at it closer, he told himself. Force yourself, use your own powers, you can't just flop down and give up.

He read and reread the descriptions—"the order of *ischim*, lower angels, men spirits"—and something clicked.

"Men spirits."

What had Gretta said? Something about how the most awful and terrifying of the fallen were punished by being deprived of form, and they can survive only by inhabiting the bodies of others. Within human beings they wreaked their havoc.

She had also said—and now he remembered her words: "We know that God limited demons and made them mortal." Mortal. Didn't that mean only one thing? They could die, they *could be* killed?

The demon in the schoolteacher he'd shot—that demon didn't die. That demon, Azazel, lived on in the raven-haired girl nearby.

But demons could be killed.

Azazel was limited and mortal. Limited how?

Hobbes read around furiously in the books, looking for more characteristics of the fallen yet still mighty demon angels. Looking for the way to touch their mortality.

He found something: "Outside they can survive for one breath only."

He read it and reread it. And reacted with even greater fury. Fury for this hideous *thing*—fury that began to feel like a kind of power.

CHAPTER 51

Hobbes wanted to tear right over there as fast as he could run. Charge into her apartment and let it all out.

But he didn't; he couldn't draw any more attention to her, expose her to any more danger than he already had. Instead, he phoned.

"I killed someone," he said. "He got me to kill an innocent man."

"I know," Gretta answered. "I'm sorry."

"And after I shot him, Azazel moved to someone else."

"Are you sure," she asked, "after death?"

"Yes, after death, I *saw* it," he said. "He can move through the air or . . ." Whatever. He didn't really have a clue what the demon actually did or how.

"And I found something, too, in one of your dad's books," he said. "Get this—" He picked up one of the books and read aloud: " 'Outside'—outside the body, I guess—'they can survive for one breath only.' "

"I've heard that before," Gretta said, "but I never knew what it meant. It explains—there's a Hebrew text that explains, 'The breath can only carry them five hundred cubits.' "

"A cubit is like a distance, right?" he said.

"From your fingertip to your elbow," she said. "That's a seventh of a mile."

"Huh," Hobbes said. "So . . . like you said . . . demons are limited in certain ways."

"Yes," she said. "It sounds like you have some kind of idea."

"Maybe," he said.

"I hope so," Gretta said.

Hobbes didn't elaborate. If she was privy to even the minor details of the idea he was developing, it might endanger her. He stayed silent. Though he didn't want to hang up.

Neither did she. They were enormous comfort to each other, just being at the other end of the line.

Finally, he said, "You okay? I'll check up on you tomorrow."

"Good night, John," she said with tenderness.

"Good night," he said.

Hobbes's vortexing nightmare notwithstanding, slight smiles crept across both of their faces as they hung up.

CHAPTER 52

Hobbes woke to sunshine and the sound of birds. He was feeling better. He kept hoping he would wake up in the morning to find it was all a bad dream; he was just a working-stiff cop grinding away at the usual slate of tawdry, depressing murder cases.

He could hear a TV cartoon playing in another part of the apartment. The reassuring sound of a normal Saturday morning. He walked out of his room with a smile, headed for the kitchen.

He went about his morning ritual. He turned on the small TV in the kitchen: a commercial for a jet ski with lots of sun and fun.

He dumped about so much coffee into the filter basket, his idea of measuring. Filled up the coffee machine with water and turned it on. He listened to the sounds from the living room as he grabbed his orange juice from the refrigerator. Sam was watching *Scooby-Doo*.

He stuck his head in the living room. "Mornin' Sam," he said.

Sam was sitting on the floor in front of the couch, absorbed in the cartoon and didn't hear.

"Good mornin', Sam," Hobbes said louder.

"Oh, hi, Unc," Sam said, looking up.

Hobbes started to leave.

"Hey, was that you last night?" Sam asked.

"How do you mean?" Hobbes said, coming back in the room.

"Somebody was doin' something funny in my sleep," Sam said. "Tickling my chest."

"You musta been dreaming," Hobbes said. He grinned and walked down the hall toward the bathroom.

On the kitchen television the commercial ended and a news report came on. It was coverage of the shooting death of the schoolteacher the night before. But it was listed as breaking news. The new information concerned a witness who had stepped forward to tell a different story from the one reported originally. This was a raven-haired sixteen-year-old girl. She was contradicting earlier witnesses who said the dead man shot first. She was pointing the finger straight at Hobbes.

Hobbes just missed hearing the report. He walked down the hall toward the bathroom, passing one of the windows he had carefully checked the night before. He didn't notice now, but the window was cracked open.

He went into the bathroom and grabbed his toothbrush off the sink ledge. He squeezed out toothpaste and brushed his teeth while leaning over and turning on the shower. He pulled off his T-shirt, ready for a relaxing steam once the water was hot. He reached in and checked the water. It was getting there. He stripped off his shorts and straightened up, catching sight of himself in the mirror for the first time.

He froze.

Stared in fear.

Written backward on the mirror in some kind of

marker were three printed letters. Reversed in reflection on Hobbes's chest they spelled, C-A-L.

Hobbes yanked on his shorts and hurtled out of the bathroom. Sprinting down the hall, he now noticed the window that had been cracked open.

As he ran past the kitchen, he caught a glimpse of the black-haired sixteen-year-old being interviewed on TV. He knew instantly and without a doubt what she was saying.

He ran into the living room and grabbed Sam, hurriedly unbuttoning the boy's pajama top.

It was as he dreaded. Printed on Sam's chest in magic marker was a letter. The letter Y with a question mark.

Sam looked down. "Why'd you write that, Unc?" he said. He smiled, thinking it was a joke of some kind.

"Where's your dad?" Hobbes said.

"In the bedroom," Sam said. "He's a sleepyhead."

Hobbes whipped his head around and fixed on the clock. 9:30. Seeing the time, he *knew*, instantly.

Unhurriedly, in order not to alarm the boy, Hobbes walked out of the room. He went straight to Art and Sam's bedroom.

It was dark, the shades still drawn. He saw Art in his bed in silhouette, lying on his side, turned away from the door.

Hobbes crossed the room to the bed, moved around the far side and knelt. He touched Art's neck, feeling for the pulse. He kept his fingers there for long moments, hoping. Then his head drooped.

He gently pulled the covers back. He saw that Art's pajama top was unbuttoned. He lifted the flap that was hanging down. Yes, as he expected. There were letters written on Art's chest: P-S-E.

Hobbes stared at the lettering. Gazed at his beloved and twice-cursed brother's face. He put his hand on Art's cheek and held it there as though to comfort him, let him know his brother's love did not stop with death. The full weight of his grief welled into tears. He lowered his head—

And saw on the floor, in a streak of daylight streaming in under the edge of the window shade, a syringe.

He picked it up, sniffed the end of the needle and stared at the thing. The implement that had taken his precious brother from him. He turned it this way and that, noting it was still a third filled with liquid.

In that instant, with that instrument in his hand, a vague and general idea he'd been harboring began to take clearer definition in his head. And an impulse and desire sharpened into an enraged and deadly resolve.

He kissed Art's head and walked to the door. He turned and looked back for a long moment on his brother, who could just as easily have been sleeping peacefully in his bed.

He closed the door silently and moved down the hall. As he walked into the kitchen, he saw a second witness on the TV news report talking about him. It was an older man telling how Hobbes had shot first, how the schoolteacher never had a chance.

The phone rang.

Hobbes spun on the phone in rage: Azazel calling him now. *Now!* He snatched up the instrument. "Hello!"

"Hey," a friendly voice said. "You see the news?" It was Jonesy.

"I'm just watching it now," Hobbes said.

"There's more," Jonesy said after a beat. "Our

friend Lou is coming to get you, bring you down for some conversation.''

In the background on Jonesy's end, Hobbes could hear another voice. ''Where's the car?'' said the voice.

It was Stanton's.

''Are they getting close?'' Hobbes heard him say. ''Who the fuck is on the radio here?''

''Gotta go,'' Jonesy said quickly and hung up.

Hobbes glanced into the living room at Sam. He snapped off the kitchen TV and hurried toward the back of the apartment.

CHAPTER 53

Hobbes dressed quickly. He slammed a number of essentials into his duffel: cell phone, his personal .38 pistol, some of Milano's books, his notebook. And the syringe that killed Art, carefully wrapped in a towel.

He went quietly into Sam and Art's room and rested his duffel on Sam's bureau. He stuffed as many of the boy's clothes as he could in the bag, as well as an extra pair of sneakers and his baseball glove.

He walked out of the room and closed the door gently behind him. He went into the living room with a handful of Sam's clothes.

Sam, still watching cartoons, looked up.

"Put these on," Hobbes said.

"Why?" Sam said. He didn't move from his seat on the rug, but his antennae went up instantly at the tone of Hobbes's voice.

"Just get dressed, okay?" Hobbes said. "Please."

Sam started getting dressed, never taking his eyes off Hobbes. Something was up, no doubt about it.

Hobbes moved to the front window. He saw Lou's unmarked work car approaching.

He turned and sprinted out of the living room, along the hallway, down the stairs. He ran to the front door and opened it, leaving it ajar. He ran back up the stairs.

As he came into the living room, Sam was knotting his sneakers. "Let's go," Hobbes said. He grabbed the duffel and handed Sam his coat. "Here, put this on," he said, leading the way out of the living room and down the hall.

He pushed up the hall window and quickly put his own coat on.

"What are we doing?" Sam asked.

"Playing a trick on somebody," Hobbes said, holding the sash up, motioning for Sam to climb out.

Sam was dubious. "Oh," he said, looking around toward the closed door of the bedroom. "What about my dad? Why aren't we—?"

"He needs some extra sleep," Hobbes said. "Here, let me help you." He boosted Sam out the window and climbed after him.

Lou and his partner, Harris, a sallow-faced man of few words, got out of their brown work car and approached Hobbes's building.

"Sometimes it ain't so pleasant bein' a cop, is it?" Lou said as they mounted the stoop. Harris said nothing. Lou wore a slight smirk.

Lou ran his finger down the names on the intercom, looking for Hobbes's buzzer. Harris just pushed on the unlatched door and walked in.

Hobbes and Sam crossed the roof, climbed down to a utility shed in back and jumped down to the alley. They ran along the alley, Hobbes looking back to see if they were being followed.

Sam liked this, skanking around like fugitives. Hobbes was grim and wary. Sam was into the game.

They emerged onto the street in back and fled down it half running, half fast walking. Hobbes looked back again and led them across the street and down the avenue toward the el stop.

As they came within sight of the three-tiered stairs up to the train station, Hobbes checked again to the rear.

Now somebody *was* there, a thickset man in a blue-black parka, and he was following them, his eyes never leaving them.

The man wasn't hurrying, but he was coming on. Hands in pocket, striding in pursuit.

Hobbes knew without an iota of doubt. It wasn't a cop, it wasn't the authorities, it was the demon. Blank-faced, single-minded.

Hobbes grabbed Sam's hand and they ran. Ran along the street and up the train station stairs three at a time.

Behind them the blank-faced man kept coming, not running, just walking with long, relentless strides. The man turned onto the stairs and mounted them two at a time. Steadily, inexorably, like a horrible fate.

A train was in the station, loading passengers. Hobbes and Sam ran to catch it. They got to the last car in time; they slipped on board and looked back.

The man was coming up the last of the stairs onto the platform. He strode after them, coming right for the train. Still he didn't run.

The doors hissed and closed.

The man kept coming.

The train lurched and started to move.

The man's pace didn't quicken or slacken; he kept on.

The train picked up speed and rolled toward the

track at the end of the station. Hobbes and Sam watched from a rear window.

The man jumped down on the tracks and kept walking, walking, stride upon stride in their wake. Undeterred, undiscouraged. To Hobbes it was an absurd yet terrifying sight. An image that said: I don't even have to try. Wherever you go, I will find you.

CHAPTER 54

Hobbes and Sam found seats halfway along the car. Hobbes plopped down with a sigh. For a moment he could relax. He patted Sam's knee; we're okay.

Sam was plenty okay. He was psyched. He never doubted they'd get away—from whoever was after them. He was with Uncle John, after all. Uncle John was pretty much infallible in Sam's eyes, especially when it came to cop stuff and bad guys.

Hobbes was scanning the length of the car, looking for any sign of trouble.

Across the train a small Polish woman in a purple bandanna was staring at Hobbes. Their eyes met. She hastily looked away.

Hobbes saw recognition in them. The TV, the news reports.

He glanced around again.

Nobody else had picked up on him. All the other passengers were staring dully out the windows or at the middle distance, where their own thoughts were hovering.

Hobbes noticed a nun several seats down.

He stared at her, thinking. He pulled out his notepad and pen and slowly wrote: 18 - 2 - APO - CAL - Y - PSE.

It was the sum of the messages, in order delivered,

everything Azazel had caused to be written. First on
the chests of Muskavich and Noons, then on the chest
of the schoolteacher Hobbes had killed. Finally, on
Hobbes's mirror and the chests of Hobbes's family.

He wrote the numbers and letters in order of appearance and read what they said. Then he re-
ordered them: "APOCALYPSE 18, 2."

He looked over at the nun again. He turned to
Sam and motioned for him to follow. He got up, and
they both moved toward where the nun was sitting.

As they got up, the Polish woman whispered
sharply to the middle-aged nurse sitting next to her.
The nurse glanced at Hobbes, met his eyes and
looked down. She looked sideways at the Polish
woman and gave a shrug: none of my business.

Hobbes bent and whispered to Sam, "Get ready
to move."

Then he crouched and sat on the edge of the seat
next to the nun. "Excuse me, Sister," he said. "Can
you tell me something?"

The nun looked at Hobbes benignly. No smile or
frown, practiced neutrality. Switzerland.

"Does the word 'Apocalypse' mean anything to
you?" he said. "I mean in the Bible?"

The train rolled into a station, its brakes squealing.
There were a good number of people waiting to
get on.

The nun looked at Hobbes for another neutral beat,
then went back to reading the tabloid daily she had
open on her lap. As though Hobbes had been talking
to someone else entirely.

The doors opened, and a dozen or so passengers
got off.

Hobbes glanced around. Now several of the remaining people were watching him.

New passengers got on. A young guy with a back-pack sat down across from Hobbes and looked at him with half recognition, trying to place his face.

The eyes of the Polish woman and the nurse both were boring holes in Hobbes's face.

The doors cleared.

"Thank you, Sister," Hobbes said to the remote and unhelpful woman of God.

He squeezed Sam's hand. Together they bolted for the closing doors. They slipped through onto the platform.

Hobbes breathed a sigh as the train pulled away. They turned toward the stairs leading down to the street. Then he stopped breathing. A transit cop was no more than thirty yards away, walking right toward them.

Hobbes grabbed Sam's hand and turned them both in the other direction. "Fast but not too fast," he said to Sam. They walked briskly, but no faster than the other passengers toward another exit.

Hobbes glanced back casually. The transit cop was still coming their way, but just walking, not hurrying. It was impossible to say if he had spotted them or was following.

Hobbes and Sam blended in among the other train riders as they all funneled toward the stairway. They took the stairs down to the middle level. Hobbes led the way around to the left, where they joined a flow of passengers heading toward another stairs.

When they got opposite a newsstand, Hobbes glanced over and there was another transit cop, and this one was facing right toward them.

No changing direction now; too suspicious. No place to hide. Hobbes turned his face away from the cop toward Sam and led the boy on a diagonal to a cluster of people at the newsstand. He slipped in behind a tall man who was buying a handful of magazines. The man's height shielded Hobbes from the view of the second transit cop.

"What's it gonna be?" said the cigar-chewing vendor, looking up at Hobbes.

Hobbes, out of past habit, grabbed a pack of cigarettes from the display and tossed down a $5 bill. "Keep the change," he said, turning away. The vendor took zero notice of Hobbes and looked around for the next customer.

Hobbes glanced past the tall man, looking for the transit cop. No sign of him. The way appeared to be clear. He took Sam's hand and guided him off in the same direction they had started out.

"Detective Hobbes? Is that you?"

Hobbes stopped.

The transit cop slid out from behind a pillar where he was hiding. He stood right in front of them.

Hobbes had no choice, he decked him. He sure as hell couldn't go downtown for some "conversation," not now.

"Run!" he said to Sam, and the two of them sprinted off down the corridor.

Behind them the transit cop pulled himself off the ground and wrenched his walkie-talkie free. He yelled into it: "All units in the area! Wanted for assault on a police officer: Detective John Hobbes. Black male, six feet tall, thirty-five years old. Suspect is with a boy, ten years old. Suspect also wanted on suspicion of murder."

CHAPTER 55

Hobbes and Sam hot-footed it down another set of stairs to the street.

They turned right on the broad, busy sidewalk and ran, dodging around other pedestrians. They had a good head start.

There was a corner coming up, a street Hobbes knew crossed under the tracks and into a farmers' market kind of place on the other side. They could disappear there in the narrow aisles and crowds.

A big truck pulled out of a transit maintenance garage ahead of them and stopped across the sidewalk for traffic to clear.

Blocked.

They could run into the street and be seen. Or—they could dash under the rapidly closing gate into the garage. They dashed under the gate and disappeared from view . . .

Just as two transit cops tore down the stairs from the train station, looking in all directions. No Hobbes or Sam. Sirens sounded in the distance, reinforcements coming.

A deactivated underground subway station housed a population of the homeless, addicts, runaways and the mildly to severely mentally ill—refuse from the government's enlightened deinstitutionalization social policy of the early eighties.

Now the abandoned subway station at 30th and Corcoran was temporary safe haven for two more of society's undesirables, the fugitive Hobbes and his nephew, Sam.

Hobbes led Sam to one side of the cavernous space, at a distance from the encampments of oil-drum fires and foul-mouthed gesticulating tenants.

They found a place to sit by a concrete installation housing electrical conduits.

They sat for a while in silence. There were things to say to Sam, but Hobbes didn't have a clue where to start.

Sam was cool; he figured Hobbes would tell him what was going on at the right time.

Hobbes fished out his notebook and jotted something down in it. He put it away in his pocket. More silence.

Hobbes tried his cell phone; it didn't work. When he shoved the phone back in his coat pocket, he found the pack of cigarettes he had bought. He took the cigarettes out and looked at them for a moment.

"I thought you quit," Sam said. "I thought they were bad for you."

"They are," Hobbes said. He put the pack away. More silence. The weight of the situation was falling heavier on Hobbes with each lengthening moment of inactivity.

Finally, Hobbes could put it off no longer. "Sam," he said, "do you know what's happening?"

Sam shook his head no.

"The police think I did some very bad things," Hobbes said.

"You *are* the police," Sam said.

"Not now, I'm not," Hobbes said.

"Well, why do they think you . . ." Sam trailed off, fidgeting. Wondering: Hobbes not the police?

" 'Cause someone's making it look that way," Hobbes said.

Sam was quiet. Then: "I saw that once on a show."

Hobbes nodded. He let the silence lengthen again, then went for it. "I have to talk to you about something else," he said.

Sam tensed slightly. He didn't look at Hobbes. Whenever a grown-up said they had to talk about "something" instead of just talking about it, that meant bad news was coming.

"Your dad," Hobbes said.

Sam stared at him.

Hobbes lowered his eyes. How could he begin to say this?

"He's not asleep, is he?" Sam said.

"No," Hobbes said.

Sam nodded. He gave no visible emotional response. He stared across the space at the flickering fires. "Did it hurt?" he asked.

"I don't think so," Hobbes said.

Sam nodded again. He was glad for that. He sat silently as a train roared by. "Tell me something," Sam said. "Do you think he's going to heaven?"

"Well, if anybody's goin'," Hobbes said, "it'll be your dad."

Sam thought about that. "That's what I think, too," he said.

Then, ever practical as kids are about the important things, he turned to Hobbes and said, "What happens now? Where'm I gonna go? What'm I gonna do?"

"You'll be okay," Hobbes said.

Sam smiled slightly. He reached out and took Hobbes's hand. "You and me," he said, "we're a team, right?"

Hobbes nodded with a small smile. Then he had to look away. He had a plan, and the plan didn't call for a team.

CHAPTER 56

They stayed hidden there for several hours until Hobbes felt it was probably safe.

They got to their feet and circumnavigated the outlanders on their way to the sunken rail right-of-way, which was the only exit from the blocked-off station. They pulled back to avoid the powerful headlight of an oncoming express, turning away as it flashed past.

They trudged along the tracks to the next station, which was in active use.

Hobbes watched the platform from a distance until it was almost empty of people and there were no transit cops in sight. He and Sam hurried up from the tracks and headed for the stairs at the far end of the station.

There was one street exit to this station. When they sprinted up the stairs and reached the doors, Hobbes hesitated, held Sam back, and cracked open the doors with one hand.

On the street just outside the station was a construction zone. Workers, sawhorse barriers, a big compressor and a cement mixer formed a maze they'd have to thread through. On the street side of this obstacle course was a cop directing traffic.

Hobbes drew back inside. They'd have to skulk

around inside the station until the cop took a break or went home for the night.

Hobbes and Sam didn't get to Gretta's tree-lined street until after dark. They walked past the front entrance and down a side alley to a fire escape. They climbed up it as quietly as possible.

At the living room window Hobbes peered in and saw Gretta in her bathrobe across the way in the kitchen, making herself a cup of tea. He screwed up his courage and tapped on the window.

Gretta whirled, frightened.

Hobbes spoke quickly through the six-inch space open at the bottom of the window. "It's me," he said. "I tried to call, but your line was busy."

Gretta exhaled in relief. She approached the window, but still with a touch of trepidation. Was it the actual Hobbes? Or—?

"I'm sorry," Hobbes said. "We had no place else to go."

She nodded, hugging her bathrobe around her. But she did not open the window.

Hobbes watched her face carefully. "This is my nephew, Sam," he said.

"Hi, Sam," she said.

Still she hesitated, not sure.

In a move meant to reassure, Hobbes stuck his hand a little way through the opening. He couldn't have known, but the gesture caused Gretta to flash back terrified to the gray-haired man reaching through the revolving door, grabbing at her. She shivered.

She steeled herself. This *was* the real Hobbes, and his gesture meant something else. "Touch me. Trust me. Trust I'm not bearing the demon," Hobbes said.

She made the leap of faith. She looked at his face, smiled almost wistfully and raised her hand toward his. As their palms met and their fingers folded over each other's, she had the feeling she was joining her fate to his. For better or worse.

They came around the building, and she let them in through the front door.

As Sam came in, she squatted down to his level and smiled. "I'm Gretta," she said. "It's really good to meet you, Sam."

He looked her over and gave her a shy smile. "You're in your pajamas," he said.

She laughed. "Well, I wasn't expecting company," she said. And added quickly, "But I'm glad to have you here."

Sam looked around self-consciously at her place. All the angels started to register. His eyes widened. He moved past her into the living room, scouting the place out.

Hobbes spoke to Gretta. "Azazel wrote on his chest," he said, low. "Unless I do something, he's next."

She nodded, pained for him. "I'm sorry about your brother," she said.

"Yeah," Hobbes said. "He was an innocent."

He moved past her and looked out the front window. "Azazel and the entire city are looking for us," he said.

Gretta watched him for a moment. "Just like my dad," she said.

He turned toward her. "Hey. Look," he said, "if you don't want us to—"

"It's okay," she said softly. "You can stay here." She had already made the choice; she had crossed the bridge.

"Thanks," Hobbes said. "He'll take the couch. I'll take the rug."

She considered that. And nodded. "He'll take the couch."

CHAPTER 57

It had started snowing. The quiet, floating straight down kind that cleanses the air, leaves a fresh smell and seems to bestow a blessing for the whole time of its pristine fall.

Hobbes watched from the living room window, mentally hashing and rehashing his few options. None of them would look good when the snow melted away, he knew. If he had the guts to do what he wanted—and if he could figure out how—it would look like the act of a madman. Another "normal" guy who snapped. No one would know what his real choices had been.

Almost no one.

He went and sat on the coffee table next to where Sam was sleeping on the couch. He smoothed the boy's hair and touched his cheek.

Gretta came from the kitchen and brought Hobbes a cup of coffee. She sank into an armchair next to the two of them.

They sat for long minutes watching Sam's sleeping form. The boy was oblivious, breathing easily. It was for Sam and his children's children that these adults had to agonize in the night, that decisions had to be taken.

Hobbes got up and went to Gretta's desk. He sat

and unfolded the paper on which he had written the inscription: APOCALYPSE 18, 2. He smoothed out the paper and opened one of Gretta's Bibles.

He ran his finger down the list of books in the Bible—the table of contents. No book named Apocalypse.

He rose and took down two other versions of the Bible from a shelf.

He checked the table of contents of one of them and found nothing. He checked the third. He ran his finger down the list of books. At Revelation it said in small type beneath the name: "Apocalypse was the Greek word for Revelation."

Hobbes dove into the Bible, flipping pages until he found Revelation 18, 2.

It read: "Babylon the great is fallen, is fallen, and has become a dwelling place of demons."

He took the Bible over to Gretta, who was about to doze off in the armchair next to Sam on the couch. He read her the lines.

She cocked her head. "We believe," she said, "they have a larger malicious purpose. They want to cause the fall of civilization."

"The fall of Babylon as they put it," Hobbes said.

"They have a master plan," she said. "Reese, the murderer my father caught—both of them were extremely comfortable hosts for Azazel, human wastelands. Not a lot of moral fiber left. They were true homes for him, where he could thrive and do a lot of damage. They were prime agents, so to speak."

"Meant for larger things?" Hobbes asked.

She nodded. "They were beings who were capable of spreading evil wider," she said. "Reese fomenting Arab rage against the Jews."

She frowned and went on. "We think Reese was

also a 'multiplier'—a propagator. They expected him to be fruitful and multiply. The millennium is on us, the time is ripe in the world."

"All the wars," Hobbes said. "Ethnic cleansing, Zaire, famine, AIDS. They're on a roll."

"And we're getting in the way," she said.

Hobbes stared at her for a long beat.

He cursed softly to himself and paced and sat again at the desk and mulled over her remarks. He fidgeted with the pack of cigarettes. He looked up from the Bible passage and tore open the cigarettes. He knocked one out and stared at it.

He got up again, went into the kitchen and poured himself another cup of coffee. He read from his notebook and thought deeply. This would be a one-shot deal. There would be no going back if he got it wrong.

He stared up at a pair of angels flanking the wall clock. He went back to Gretta. She was staring at him wide-eyed this time, expecting something.

"I want to make sure I'm thinking this through," he said to her.

She nodded.

"Demons can only live in the bodies of other beings," he said. "And when its host body dies, the demon can survive for one breath only."

"And can only go 500 cubits," Gretta said.

"Yes," Hobbes said, thinking. "But he also told me, Azazel said: When he 'moves as spirit, no man can resist.'"

"That makes an odd kind of sense," Gretta said. "People of character can resist the touch. But when the demon is out of body, desperate, fighting for *his* life, he's stronger."

Hobbes nodded. How many thousands of years

had the demon survived this way? How many bodies had he inhabited?

Hobbes knew what he needed to know. He knew what his choice had to be.

CHAPTER 58

Hobbes emptied Sam's stuff out of his duffel bag and piled it on the table. Through the open door of the bedroom he could see Gretta lying asleep in her bed.

He moved quietly into the kitchen and poured fresh coffee into a Thermos. He took it back to the living room and put it into the duffel bag, along with his notebook, his .38, a couple of Milano's books and the wrapped-up towel.

He took his pack of unused cigarettes from the table and put it in the pocket of his brown leather jacket.

He lay the jacket across the duffel bag and moved into the bedroom.

He looked down at Gretta asleep. What a strange hand life had dealt him. To find such a woman at this stage of things. To spin into the orbit of someone who could, under different circumstances, so easily be everything a man wanted and needed in a companion; only to be cast by fate into the cold.

He sat gently on the edge of the bed. Gretta's eyes opened.

"I have to know that whatever happens, you and Sam are safe," he said.

She nodded.

"Take him somewhere," he said, "somewhere no one knows about."

"Okay," she said. "I know a place in—"

Hobbes cut her off sharply. "Don't tell me," he said.

She nodded. She raised one hand for him to take. He folded her hand in his. After a moment he lay down next to her, his back to her. They spooned.

With his face hidden from her, he let his expression go for a few moments—the weight of everything that had happened and would happen.

"I'm scared, Gretta," he said. "I'm really scared."

At dawn Hobbes sat up from a fitful few hours of sleep. He pulled on his shoes and washed his face and had a cup of coffee. He went into the living room and sat down on the couch next to Sam.

He looked up at the prints of angels above the boy. He reached out and took his hand.

Sam half woke up.

"Sam, I have to go," Hobbes said.

Sam's eyes opened a little further.

"You're gonna stay with Gretta for a while," Hobbes said. "Maybe a long while. When she thinks it's time, she'll take you to Nana's."

Sam looked past Hobbes. Gretta stood in the bedroom doorway in her pajamas and robe. She smiled reassuringly.

"I want you to know," Hobbes said, "whatever people say, whatever I do . . . I'm doing it for you, okay? Because I love you."

Sam looked up at him blankly, staring for a long moment. He realized somewhere in his consciousness he was hearing something of great importance, but he wasn't ready to deal with it. If Uncle John was arranging things, he knew he'd be okay. That's all he could manage right now. It was practically the middle of the night; he was wiped.

"I'm going back to sleep," he said to Hobbes and closed his eyes. "And when I wake up, everything's going to be just the way it was."

That almost broke Hobbes's heart. He looked up at Gretta. "You sure it's okay," he said to her softly.

She nodded. Firmly. She had made her decision. There was no going back.

Hobbes got up and moved away from the couch with her. He dug out his notebook and held it out to her. "You might be able to use this," he said.

She took it with interest, opened it, leafed through some pages. She saw what it was, nodding as she read.

Hobbes watched her. "You know what this means, right?" he said.

What it meant for Gretta was something huge. It meant no more hiding. It meant the likelihood of full engagement. It meant taking on the adversary for real, not just reading about him, not just exchanging cryptic phone calls with other postulants in Stockholm or Budapest. Preparing in the abstract was over.

"I'm ready," she said with a slightly ironic look.

Hobbes grabbed up his duffel bag.

They walked to the door together and hugged. Hobbes opened the door into the hall and stepped halfway through. He turned and took her hand and squeezed it. He looked from her face, from her clear, brave, frightened eyes to a picture of an angel on the wall. "They don't all have wings, you know," he said.

She held his hand to her face.

A long moment.

Slowly, he pulled his hand away, stepped past the door and pulled it closed behind him.

CHAPTER 59

He was on the expressway headed out of town. In Gretta's dark blue Volvo sedan. He drove right at the speed limit and made sure not to overtake any car that might be a police car.

He checked his watch and calculated the minimum time he needed.

He pulled his cell phone out of his duffel bag and punched some numbers.

A voice answered: "Precinct." It was Denise.

"Hey, Denise," Hobbes said matter-of-factly. "Can I have Jonesy?"

A beat. Two beats.

He was connected.

"Hey," Jonesy said.

"Hey," Hobbes said.

"Where are you?" Jonesy said.

"Yeah, right," Hobbes said sarcastically. "Who else is on the line? Lou? Stanton? Hi, guys."

"You gotta come in, Hobbes," Jonesy said. "Really. You can beat this thing."

Hobbes said nothing.

"I'm worried," Jonesy said. "Wachoo gonna do, where you gonna go?"

"Nowhere," Hobbes said. "I'm gonna take a long

drive, go where no one'll find me. Sit by the water and think."

As you read this you must be wondering what I'm doing? "Azazel" will enter every cop on the force until he finds this out! Isn't that obvious?!
Of course. That's the idea.
But I have to be careful. Very careful . . .

Hobbes changed lanes and positioned himself to take the spur to the northern interstate at the next interchange. He kept the cell phone to his ear, checking his watch.

"Hey, Hobbes, I gotta ask you something," Jonesy said.

Hobbes reflexively checked his rearview mirror, not expecting to find anything. Instead, he saw a police black-and-white two cars back.

"Shoot," Hobbes said.

"We been partners a long time," Jonesy said.

The one car between Hobbes and the black-and-white chose now to pull out and pass. The cop car was right behind him.

"Twelve plus," Hobbes said.

Hobbes saw the signs for Interstate North coming up. He checked his rearview: The black-and-white was closing the distance between them. The two cops' heads seemed to be riveted on Hobbes's car.

"So," Jonesy said. "Is there anything you wanna tell me?"

It was an invitation to confess. He knew Jonesy was obliged to go that route.

"Yeah," Hobbes said. He put on his signal to follow the Northway branch to the right. The cops stayed right behind him, inching closer, as though ready to pull him over. "Remember our talk the other night?" he went on. "When the moment comes, you know it."

The black-and-white suddenly veered left and sped off down the expressway. Hobbes continued on straight up the Northway.

"Hey," Jonesy said with real concern, "be careful, partner. I'll see you, huh?"

Hobbes knew he meant he was pretty sure he'd never see him again.

"Yeah," Hobbes said.

Hobbes hung up. A fresh fall of snow flared across his windshield.

He turned on the car's heater and reached into the duffel bag for the Thermos of coffee.

At the precinct Jonesy hung up his desk phone and looked across the room at Stanton, who of course had been listening in on the conversation.

Jonesy shrugged. Stanton shrugged back, a sour look on his face. Jonesy was silently pleased they had found out nothing of substance.

So he thought.

CHAPTER 60

Snow blanketed the roadsides and shrouded the mountain pines.

The snowstorm had passed, the road itself was open, the sky was clearing.

A pale three-quarter moon hung over the ridge tops as Hobbes inched Gretta's Volvo up the long gradual inclines. The last few miles were especially lonely ones; not a car in either direction for the final half hour as Hobbes drove toward Milano's remote hideaway.

He found the entrance to the driveway and turned down it. The wheels crunched through untracked snow and gravel toward the cabin.

Hobbes braked the car to a stop within the canopy of the woods, some two hundred feet back from the little house.

He got out. And reached back in and took his gun, Gretta's thermos and one other thing from the duffel bag, the syringe wrapped in the towel. He stuck them in the pockets of his jacket.

He closed the car door and walked away, turning to throw the car keys into the night. They landed somewhere in the dark, in the snow at the base of some bushes off the road.

He turned back and made his way across the frozen rutted driveway toward the cabin.

You're probably wondering what I'm doing. Well, this is where things got tricky.

It was just him and me now, Hobbes and Azazel.

I thought I had him. This was it. It was going to work out exactly as planned.

And he thought he had me.

Hobbes pushed the front door open and entered the cabin.

The first thing he saw in the reflected moonlight were the remnants of the taped outline of Milano's body on the kitchen floor.

He gathered kindling, broke up some old pieces of deck furniture and made a fire in the fireplace.

When it was roaring good, sending crimson daggers pulsing across the walls and ceiling, he sat by the front window. He drank coffee from his thermos and waited.

Lest his resolve waver, he ran the movie of Sam's life in front of his mind's eye. From Sam's birth through the day of Art's accident to the day father and son moved in with him; through the swift-flowing days and nights of Sam's boyhood, while his Uncle John watched him growing into a little man.

Lest his resolve waver . . .

Lights flashed back in the trees.

Headlights lasered through openings between the pines and maples as a car turned onto the winding entrance road and moved toward him.

CHAPTER 61

The headlights went out. The faint sound of the car engine continued.

A hundred yards away, the engine noise ceased.

Hobbes got to his feet, armed himself with his handgun and went to the front door. He stepped out on the stoop. There he stood silhouetted in the firelight, waiting.

To a pair of eyes moving through the woods, Hobbes was a spooky sight, immobile in the doorway. Broad-shouldered and erect. Waiting for his destiny. Menacing.

Hobbes's shout came echoing across the cold night. "Come on out!" his voice rang on the empty air. "I know you're here! I knew you'd come!"

Silence.

"*Innah yahdah-hahnah d'minnou aht!*" Hobbes shouted. "I know who you are!"

The eyes in the woods moved silently, shifting to the side, gliding like a shark.

"What do you want now?" Hobbes called.

The eyes moved forward through the trees, closer, as though stalking.

"Haven't you done enough!" came Hobbes's voice.

Across the clearing on the other side of the driveway, another pair of eyes.

These were moving forward toward the cabin also, triangulating Hobbes, pinioning him against the shimmering garish firelight.

Hobbes, massive and solid against the shifting light, was not going to move. "You made me kill an innocent man!" he shouted. "You *murdered* my brother! What more do you want? How much 'fun' can you have?"

A figure stepped into view from behind a pine. Stanton, shivering in his topcoat, hands stuck in his pockets. "What're you talking about, Hobbes? I didn't do any of that stuff. I just want to bring you in, okay?"

Hobbes turned to face the lieutenant coming toward him. "So it's you," Hobbes said.

"Yeah, it's me," Stanton said with a look that said: Who'd you expect, Michael Jordon? "Put the gun down. I know you got one."

"Or else what?" Hobbes said. "You'll shoot me? Where's the fun in that?"

Stanton stopped his forward advance, stood hunched with his hands in his coat pockets; pained and pissed off. "Fuck you, huh?" he said. "*You*'re making me do this! Just drop the goddamn gun!"

That sure sounded like Stanton, Hobbes was thinking. He debated, uncertain.

"Do what he says, Hobbes," a voice from the left said.

Hobbes whirled.

A hulking figure moved with slow steps through the snowy clearing toward him. Hobbes groaned. His heart sank. "Jonesy?" he said almost under his breath.

CHAPTER 62

Jonesy? *You're* Azazel? Hobbes thought to himself as his partner appeared. His spirits fell one more devastating notch. "Who else is out there?" he said. "Lou? Tiff?"

"Just us," Stanton said.

"The gun, Hobbes," Jonesy said.

The two policemen were on opposite sides of Hobbes, twenty yards apart.

Hobbes looked back and forth between them; they both looked and sounded like themselves. Was he insanely wrong about this whole thing? Had he simply slid over the edge into weird paranoid fantasies of demons and master plans to defeat civilization?

"Listen to me, Jonesy," he called. "I didn't do it. I didn't do any of it."

"I know that, Hobbes," Jonesy said, standing shivering in the snow thirty feet from him.

"We *both* want to believe that," Stanton said. "But we gotta bring you in."

Stalemate.

Hobbes agonized. He did as much of a reality check as he could muster. Muskavich, Noons, the man who attacked Gretta, the schoolteacher in the street, his brother, the scrawls on everybody's chests, including Sam's.

Not just his imagination.

People dead, in danger, his own career destroyed. The Robert Milano pattern to a T. He was locked in. Cornered. On the cliff edge. He had to go through with this.

"Stan," Jonesy said, turning toward the lieutenant.

"Yeah?" Stanton said.

"I don't know if I can do this," Jonesy said.

"What the fuck're you talkin'?" Stanton said with a scowl.

"Say Hobbes disappeared into the woods," Jonesy said. "We drive his car into the lake, end of story. What's wrong with that?" He was sidestepping gradually closer to Stanton as he talked, his gun out, up about half-staff in Hobbes's direction.

Stanton gave Jonesy a look. "We bring the son-of-a-bitch *in*!" Stanton said. "That's why we're here. He did it? Fine. He didn't? Even better. But it's not our job to decide."

He turned his gaze back toward Hobbes. "Now put the gun down," he said.

Hobbes looked back and forth between them, trying to tell who was who, trying to figure the odds. "Jonesy?" he said, moving a few steps away from the house.

Jonesy gave him a sad, ironic look. "Put the goddamn gun down," he said softly.

Hobbes watched both men, looking for an escape route. Maybe neither one is the demon; what then? He had to get away, stay at liberty and free to do what he had to do.

Jonesy had moved in closer and now had his service automatic casually raised and pointed pretty much in Hobbes's direction.

Hobbes had no chance to run. He held his own

gun out in front of him and, after much hesitation, dropped it to the ground.

Jonesy started to move closer and stopped. Shook his head. An odd frozen moment. He glanced toward Stanton. "I'm sorry, Stan," he said. "When you've been on the force long enough, you think you've seen it all, right? But you haven't. 'Cause life always gives you one more surprise."

He swept the gun forty-five degrees left and shot Stanton in the head. Stanton dropped like a slaughtered animal.

"Sometimes it's a big one," Jonesy said.

CHAPTER 63

Hobbes stared at Jonesy in horror and edged back toward the house, where the firelight still spiked up and down inside. "Azazel," Hobbes breathed.

"Hey, I'm your *partner*, man," Jonesy said in his easygoing way, gun in hand, gesturing with it, not exactly pointing it. "Go on, you're free. Run."

Hobbes glanced toward the woods, then quickly back at "Jonesy." He kept backing up toward the house. If he ran, wouldn't Jonesy/Azazel just shoot him in the back?

"Keep thinking, Hobbes," Jonesy said with a slight smile. He raised the pistol deliberately and fired. A bullet tore into the ground between Hobbes's feet.

Hobbes leapt backward. Jonesy fired again. The pine log next to Hobbes's head splintered. Hobbes jumped inside the house.

"Jonesy" laughed and started ambling around the outside of the house. "You see it," said the voice coming out of Jonesy. "Now Jonesy's fucked, too. He just shot his boss. *You're* fucked, *Jonesy's* fucked. One at a time, eh? That's how we do it. One by one . . ."

"Jonesy" moved around the house toward the back door. Very casually, he leaned down and glanced in each of the windows as he came to them. He didn't try to shield himself; as though he didn't care if he got shot.

"Olee-olee-oxen-free!" he sang through the broken screen of the open back door. He looked as if he expected Hobbes to come out.

When Hobbes didn't emerge, "Jonesy" began a song: "Time . . . is on my side . . . Yes it is . . ."

He continued around the house, casing the place, looking for Hobbes. "See the deal?" he said. "I kill you, it's the final pathetic chapter in the life of another disgraced hero. You're just one more piece-of-shit human scum."

He came around to the front of the cabin again. "Or, turn it around," he said cheerfully. "If *I* die, I'll enter you! And before you go down, I'll put twenty more murders on your tab. Maybe your nephew!" He chuckled heartily at his genius. "And that chippie you were talking to."

"Jonesy" was tripping lightly with his ideas, riffing on the delicious possibilities. He loved this shit. "Which way to go, huh?" he said, his eyes dancing with anticipation. "You die or I die? What's maximum fun?"

Standing opposite the front door, he faced inward, calling to Hobbes, "Can you guess—can you?—what *maximum* fun is?" He gave a loud laugh and said portentously, "Sure you can."

He raised his pistol and moved it slowly, inexorably, toward his own temple. "Now that I've played you from the *out*side," he said, "maximum fun is"—he paused for dramatic effect—"I *become* you." He smiled broadly, pointed the barrel at his head and began to tighten his finger.

Hobbes flew from inside the cabin and knocked "Jonesy" to the ground.

They fought over "Jonesy" 's gun, rolling on the icy driveway. "Jonesy" was still trying to aim the gun, not at Hobbes, but at his own head. Hobbes struggled against that, pulling the gun lower, lower, until it disappeared between them. The gun went off.

"Jonesy" lurched backward away from Hobbes. He laughed throatily.

Hobbes rolled away, raising himself slowly up. Who took the bullet? Hobbes?

"Jonesy" pushed himself to a half-sitting position, holding his chest. "Eww, you got me, Hobbes," he said. "You got me good." He laughed painfully.

Hobbes dragged himself to his feet and retreated to the cabin steps. He sat down and put the gun on the stoop next to him.

"Jonesy" leaned back against a tree trunk, groaning. "I gotta ask you something," he said. "You wouldn't let me kill myself. Why is that?"

CHAPTER 64

"Kill yourself quick like that—bang?" Hobbes said. "No, I need more time." He looked at "Jonesy" 's gun, now by his side.

"Time for what, asshole?" the harsh Azazel voice said.

"I figured it out," Hobbes said. He reached into his coat pocket and took out a cigarette.

"Five hundred cubits," Hobbes went on. "That's a long way. If Jonesy dies too fast, as powerful as you are, I might never get away from you."

"Ooh," Azazel/Jonesy said. "He's catchin' on. What, you think you're gonna win this thing?" He coughed up some blood.

Hobbes smiled. "You never know," he said. "You never know." He lit the cigarette.

"Let me ask you something," Hobbes said. "Why do you think Milano came all the way out here in the middle of nowhere?"

"To die," the Jonesy figure said, "the little chicken shit."

"No, I don't think so," Hobbes said. "I think he wanted to do what I am *going* to do, only he couldn't pull it off."

"Pull what off?" "Jonesy" said.

"Come on, Azazel, open your eyes," Hobbes said.

"Look around sometime. Here we are, this beautiful place. Not another human being around for miles. Just you and me."

Hobbes inhaled a big breath of smoke.

"What's this?" Jonesy/Azazel said. "You don't *smoke* anymore."

"You're right, I don't," Hobbes said. "And you know why?"

"Jonesy" stared at him. He was wheezing slightly, weakening.

" 'Cause cigarettes kill," Hobbes said.

Jonesy/Azazel's expression began to darken; he was beginning to understand.

"Especially," Hobbes went on, "cigarettes laced with poison."

"Bullshit!" Azazel croaked, the voice now almost entirely his. He stopped talking, overcome by a wave of pain.

"The same poison you used to kill my brother," Hobbes said.

"Fuck you!" Azazel spat out.

"Ain't that sweet?" Hobbes said. "Ain't it just beautiful. We die together, Azazel. Just you and I." He started singing, low, grim. "Time . . . is on my side . . . Yes it is . . . yes it is . . ."

"Fuck you, motherfucker!" Azazel howled.

Hobbes reached down for the gun on the stoop and moved toward "Jonesy." "I'm sorry, Jonesy," he said. He lifted the service revolver and fired. Just once, but close and dead aim. Jonesy died instantly with a bullet in his brain.

Hobbes stared down at Jonesy's body. His friend and partner. Hobbes's mood shifted. Now he mourned his friend. Mourned the lives they'd both just lost. "I'm sorry, Jonesy," he said again, and this time his heart was sure for whom he grieved.

Hobbes looked around slowly. It was going to happen in seconds, he knew. The demon. He was waiting for him to hit. Waiting for the fate he had laid out for himself.

CHAPTER 65

Hobbes closed his eyes. His face started to sweat.

The invisible battle was joined.

The disembodied spirit scrambling for a new home. He was desperate, hugely strengthened, overwhelming.

Hobbes's breathing became harsher, more intense, his face reflecting the iron set of his will as he fought the onslaught.

He took another strong drag on his poisoned cigarette. Frowned . . . winced . . .

A violent change in his face.

He yanked the cigarette from his mouth and hurled it away in disgust. His expression turned ugly, enraged.

Hobbes had gone under.

Azazel rose ascendant.

He stumbled away from the bodies of Jonesy and Stanton, looking around with a touch of panic. His eyes landed on Gretta's blue Volvo in the distance back in the trees.

He felt for the car keys, then fell to his knees in a sudden paroxysm of pain.

He staggered back up. Felt his pockets for keys again—remembered!

Whirled toward the car, let out a howl of curses.

He made a stumbling dash for the car, toward the snowfield and bushes near it where he'd thrown the keys.

He stumbled across the icy rutted drive, lurching, clutching at his clothing. He went down on his knees, reeled up and charged on into the snowfield bordering the gravel road.

He searched around frantically with anguished eyes.

He veered and plunged into some bushes near a large fallen pine, dove into them face first. Scrabbling with his hands, clawing the ground around them, breaking branches. Searching as though his survival depended on it.

"God damn, God damn, God damn!" he cursed under his breath.

Hobbes—Azazel—was about to die.

Ferocious panicked digging, lungs straining hoarsely for any tiny breath that continued life.

He saw them—the keys! Struck at them with a desperate lunge, snagged them. He squeezed them in his fist as though to let them slip away was to lose, lose for all time.

He tried to catch his breath. Couldn't.

He tried to rise on all fours. Couldn't. He fell back into the snow and leaves.

Ha. Like I said at the start. I was beaten. Outsmarted. Poisoned . . . By John Hobbes.

Behind Hobbes's splayed, shuddering form, the shadow of the car half hidden among the trees. Hobbes yearned for it, clutching the car keys, and made one last effort to rise.

Couldn't.

He spun, fell onto his back. Hyperventilating.

That face normally handsome now ravaged, twisted in agony. He grabbed his chest

He thought of everything.
Telling Gretta to take Sam away—someplace he didn't know about. Using my poison against me. Making sure there wasn't a living human within miles.
Even throwing away his keys 'cause he knew I'd park far away. I'd want to use his car to fly.

Quiet descended, save for the rasping, slowing breath of poor doomed bastard Hobbes.
One leg continued to tremble.
Less and less.

Can you imagine what it feels like to be alive for thousands of years and realize you're actually going to die! 'Cause some self-righteous cop decided he was going to save the fucking world??!

Hobbes eyes flickered. He was fading.

Well, a demon may die, but the war isn't over, I promise you. Not by a long shot.

Hobbes breathed no more.
The lake and the little frame cabin lay still and beautiful in the moonlight.
A sudden gust of wind picked up sheets of snow and wiped them across the driveway. The snow came to rest, beginning to conceal Hobbes's form and draw chaste covers over the fallen figures of Jonesy and Stanton nearer the house.
The wind died down.
Nothing stirred.

Hobbes had won. In killing himself he had taken the demon down, too. One fewer demon, and a particularly heinous one, one that had "plans."

Expiring with the expiration of his "one breath only."

Dead.

And yet it is I who've been telling you this story.

I am Hobbes and not Hobbes. I am Azazel. I am the sum of all the humans I have inhabited.

Eons of bloody, brilliant work. And then Hobbes died and took me with him!

And yet I am telling you his story.

In the shadow of the cabin something moved. The shifting firelight?

An animal. A *cat.*

The perfect animal.

There's a reason cats are used in spells.

There's a reason cats are called "familiars" and kept by witches.

They're the one animal that can hold evil.

The cat walked out from under the cabin and past Jonesy and Stanton. It casually picked its way across the icy gravel driveway toward the snowfield.

Did you forget something?

Like all cats, this one moved with insouciant grace and confidence.

At the beginning I said I was going to tell you about "the time I almost died."

The scrawny gray cat sauntered straight for Hobbes's supine form. It stepped daintily around the body and continued on. Nonchalantly. Past the cars.

Up the driveway.

Out onto the road . . .

Oh yes.

I have games still to play. A world yet to conquer. You're going to see more of me.

You're going to see more of me than Him.

Lovely thought, huh?

The cat disappeared into the night.

Supersaturated moonlight gave the cabin and the clearing and the forest an eerie cast, like a photograhic negative.

It was no longer clear what was solid substance and what was empty form, mere ephemera of light and shadow. It was impossible to know.

The next time you're walking down the crowded streets of a city, look around.

You'll see people moving. Maybe hundreds of people. Walking, some casually, some in a hurry. Laughing with each other, or frowning, or lost in thought.

You may see that they are—idly, casually, without even knowing what they are doing—touching one another.

Look for me. I'll be there.

See you around.